E.J. Hemming

Catalogue of the Advocates' Library and Library of the Bar of Lower Canada

SALZWASSER
VERLAG

E.J. Hemming

Catalogue of the Advocates' Library and Library of the Bar of Lower Canada

Reprint of the original, first published in 1857.

1st Edition 2023 | ISBN: 978-3-37515-494-3

Verlag (Publisher): Salzwasser Verlag GmbH, Zeilweg 44, 60439 Frankfurt, Deutschland
Vertretungsberechtigt (Authorized to represent): E. Roepke, Zeilweg 44, 60439 Frankfurt, Deutschland
Druck (Print): Books on Demand GmbH, In de Tarpen 42, 22848 Norderstedt, Deutschland

CATALOGUE

OF THE

ADVOCATES' LIBRARY

AND

LIBRARY OF THE BAR OF LOWER CANADA.

SECTION OF THE DISTRICT OF MONTREAL.

COMPILED BY

E. J. HEMMING, B.C.L.,

Advocate.

MONTREAL:

PRINTED BY JOHN LOVELL, AT THE CANADA DIRECTORY OFFICE,

ST. NICHOLAS STREET.

1857.

CATALOGUE

ADVOCATES' LIBRARY AND LIBRARY OF THE BAR OF LOWER CANADA,

SECTION OF THE DISTRICT OF MONTREAL.

Author.	Subject.	Size.	No. of Vols.	Where Published.	When.	Library.	Shelf.
Adolphus & Ellis,	Reports K. B., 4 Wm. 4, (1834)—4 Vic. (1841),	8vo.	12	London,	1835—42	A.	P 1, 2
"	" Q. B., 4 Vic. (1841)—12 Vic. (1849),	8vo.	12	"	1843—51	A.	P 2
Affre,	De la Propriété des Biens Ecclésiastiques,	8vo.	1	Paris,	1837	B.	B 4
" (Archevêque de Paris,)	De l'Appel comme d'Abus,	8vo.	1	"	1845	B.	B 4
"	De l'Administration Temporelle des Paroisses,	8vo.	1	"	1845	B.	B 4
Agier,	Du Mariage,	8vo.	2	"	1801	B.	B 2
Alauzet,	Des Assurances,	8vo.	2	"	1844	B.	B 2
Allemand,	Du Mariage,	8vo.	2	"	1853	B.	C 3
Anderson,	Origin of Commerce,	4to.	4	London,	1770	A.	C 3
Angell,	On Limitation of Actions,	8vo.	1	Boston,	1829	A.	J 6
Angell & Ames,	On Corporations,	8vo.	1	"	1855	A.	K 3
Anonymous,	Abridgment of Cases in Equity,	Folio.	1	In the Savoy,	1732	A.	J 3
"	" of Statutes in force, from Magna Charta to 9 Geo. 2,	8vo.	9	London,	1730—7	A.	O 1
"	American Jurist,	8vo.	14 in 7.	Boston,	1829—35	A.	T 2
"	" (Nos. 19 to 43 inclusive),	8vo.	7	"	1833—39	A.	T 3
"	American Jurist,	8vo.	7	"	1829—32	A.	T 3
"	Angleterre Comparée, à la France,	12mo.	1	Paris,	1851	B.	T 3
"	Annual Register of History, Politics, and Literature, fr. 1758-1826,	8vo.	94	London,	1761—1851	A.	I J K L M
"	Answer to observations by Judges of C. P., for District of Quebec,	8vo.	1	London,	1790	A.	C 1
"	Attorney's Practice,	12mo.	2	"	1750	A.	L 3
"	Cabinet Lawyer,	12mo.	1	"	1853	B.	L 1
"	Cases in Chancery,	Folio.	1	In the Savoy,	1735	A.	N 6
"	Code Rural, see Boucher d'Argis,						
"	Code Civil,	18mo.	3	Paris,	1807—18	A.	F 2
"	Code des Décisions Forenses,	4to.	1	Coligny,	1612	B.	I 6
"	Code des Terriers,	18mo.	1	Paris,	1769	B.	C
"	Code Ecclésiastique,	8vo.	1	"	1792	B.	B 2
"	Code Henry,	12mo.	1	Cap Henry,	1767	A.	E 6
"	Code Noir,	24mo.	1	Paris,		B.	B 5
"	Code Matrimonial, see Camus,						
"	Commentaire sur l'Edit. portant Création des Conservateurs des Hypothèques,	18mo.	1	Avignon,	1785	A.	E 4
"	"	18mo.	1	"	1782	B.	E 5
"	Commentaire sur l'Ordonnance Civile, see Jousse,						
"	Conférences des Coutumes,	Folio.	1			A.	A 7
"	Conférences du Code civil, see de Langlade,						
"	Contrat du Mariage,	8vo.	2	Paris,	1804	A.	C 3
"	Coutume de la Mer, see Cleirac,						
"	De la Contribution à la Légitime,	18mo.	1	Paris,	1702	B.	C 3
"	Constitutions et Loix Organiques, see Fribourg,						
"	Coutume de Bretagne,	4to.	1	Nantes,	1725	A.	C 6

Author	Title	Size	Vols.	Place	Date		
Anonymous,	Coutumes, Les	Folio.	1	Paris,	1551	A.	A 7
"	Dictionnaire Universel, see Ganeau,						
"	Dictionnaire des Domaines,	4to.	3	Rouen,	1762	A.	B 6
"	Dictionnaire de Trévoux,	Folio.	8	Paris,	1771	B.	S T
"	Dictionary, Law French and Law Latin,	12mo.	1	London	1791	A.	G
"	Discours d'un Avocat Général, see de Guidau,						
"	Droit Commun des Fiefs,	18mo.	1	Paris	1776	B.	C
"	Droit Commun de la France, see Bourjon,						
"	Docket Book.	Folio.	3			A.	P 7
"	Essais de Jurisprudence, see de la Mothe,						
"	Every Man his own Lawyer,	8vo.	1	Dublin,	1776	A.	L 2
"	Jurisprudence du Parlement de Bordeaux,	4to.	2	Paris,	1824	B.	
"	Jurist,—Reports in Law and Equity—1837-1851,	8vo.	15	London,	1838—1851	A.	S T 5
"	Jurisdiction des Officiaux, (Traité de la), see Jousse,						
"	Historical Law Tracts,	8vo.	2	Edinburgh,	1758	A.	A 5
"	History of Rome,	8vo.	3	London,	1792	A.	U 5
"	Law Magazine, (Monthly Series),	8vo.	21st only	"	1839	A.	T 2
"	Legal Observer, " (Weekly "),	8vo.	24	"	1831—44	B.	T 4
"	Les Origines ou l'Ancien Gouvernement de la France, see de Buat,						
"	Magna Britannia et Hibernia,	4to.	2	In the Savoy,	1720	A.	T 4
"	Manuel de Droit de l'Etranger en Angleterre,	18mo.	1	Paris, Londres,	1852	B.	Q 7
"	Maximes Générales sur les Droits Domaniaux, see de Cabanel,						
"	Mémoire sur la Neutralité Maritime,	8vo.	1	Amsterdam,	1812	B.	B 4
"	Mémoire du Clergé de France,	8vo.	1	Paris,	1785	B.	A 5
"	Nouveau Formulaire ou Style de Procédures,	12mo.	1	Paris,	1725	B.	B 2
"	Pandectes Françaises, see Rifié-Caubray,						
"	Paraphrases de Théophile sur les Institutes de Justinien,	18mo.	2	Dublin,	1686	A.	K 2
"	Pleader's Assistant,	8vo.	1	Dublin,	1786	A.	U 5
"	De la Police, see de la Mare,						
"	Le Praticien des Juges et Consuls,	4to.	1	Paris,	1742	A.	L 3
"	Questions concernant les Substitutions, see d'Aguesseau,						
"	Recueil d'Edits,—Philippe 6,—Louis 1?,	Folio.	2	"	1720	A.	K 6
"	Recueil des Arrêts De Lamoignon,	4to.	1	"	1777	A.	F 6
"	Recueil d'Arrêts, see de Grainville.						
"	Repertorium Juridicum,	Folio.	2	In the Savoy,	1742	A.	R 7
"	Des Retraits,	8vo.	1	Paris,	1779	E.	C 4
"	Revue de Legislation, see Wolowski.						
"	Revue Critique de Législation, see do.,						
"	Revue Coloniale,	8vo.	13	"	1843—47	B.	S 3
"	" " (Deuxième Série,) 1848-51.	8vo.	6 in 4	"	1849—51	B.	S 3
"	" " " " 4 Nos. of 1852.	8vo.		"	1852	B.	S 3
"	Revised Statutes of Vermont, see Vermont,						
"	Des Sociés,	18mo.	1	Paris,	1720	B.	K 2
"	De la Souveraineté du Roy,	4to.	2	"	1755	A.	B 6
"	State Trials,—1338, (Ric. ii,)—1765, 5 (Geo. iii,)	Folio.	in 10	London,	1730—66	A.	M 7
"	State Trials,—1338, (Ric. ii,)—1765, 5 (Geo. iii.)	4to.	2	"	1773—76	A.	M ?
"	Statutes at large from Magna Charta, see United Kingdom,						
"	Statutes of Canada, see Canada,						

Author.	Subject.	Size.	No. of Vols.	Where Published.	When.	Library.	Shelf.
Anonymous,	Tarif des Douanes de France,	4to.	1	Paris,	1853	B.	B 6
Angevin,	Six Livres de la République, see Bodin,						
Anstey,	On the Queen's Supremacy,	8vo.	1	London,	1850	B.	B 3
Archbold,	Practice of Court of K. B.,	12mo.	2	"	1826	A.	L 3
"	Jervis's Acts,	12mo.	1	"	1851	B.	
"	Criminal Law, Supplement to—	8vo.	1	"	1851	B.	
"	Criminal Pleading and Evidence,	8vo.	1	"	1853	A.	
Argou,	Institution au Droit Français,	18mo.	in 2	Paris,	1771	A.	M 3
"	"	12mo.	in 2	"	1787	A.	E 3
Araould,	Système Maritime et Politique des Européens,	8vo.	1	"	1797	B.	E 3
Astruc,	Des Servitudes,	12mo.	1	Avignon,	1751	A.	A 4
Atkyns,	Chancery Reports, 7 Geo. ii, (1735-1754),	8vo.	3	London,	1781—82	B.	C 2
Aublet de Maubuy,	Des Dépôts,	18mo.	1	Paris,		A.	N 1
Augan,	Cours de Notariat,	8vo.	2	"	1846	B.	D 2
"	Arrêts Notables,	Folio.	2	"	1756	A.	K 3
Aulanier,	Du Domaine Congéable,	Folio.	2	"		B.	I 7
Auroux des Potamiers,	Coutumes de Bourbonnais,	8vo.	1	St. Brieuc,	1847	B.	I 7
Automne,	Conférence, du Droit, Français avec le Droit Romain,	Folio.	1	Paris,	1732	B.	C 2
Auzanet,	Œuvres de,	4to.	1	"	1615	B.	B 7
Aymart,	Explication de l'Ordinance de Louis XV. concernant les Substitutions,	Folio.	1	"	1708	A.	U 4 / E 7
Azuni,	Droit Maritime de l'Europe,	4to.	1	Avignon,	1754	B.	D 4
"	"	8vo.	2 in 1	Paris,	1805	B.	A 4

Author	Subject	Size	No. of Vols.	Where Published	When	Library	Shelf
Bacon,	Abridgment,	8vo.	8	London,	1832	A.	a b
"	Abridgment,	Folio.	5	"	1778	A.	P 7
"	Sur la Justice Universelle,	8vo.	1	Paris,	1824	B.	A 5
Bacquet,	Œuvres de	Folio.	2	Lyon,	1744	A.	G 7
Baker,	Office of Coroner,	12mo	1	London,	1851	B.	M 2
Bainbridge,	On Mines and Minerals,	8		London,	1841	A.	C 1
Baldwin,	British Customs,—Rates of Merchandize, 12 Charles 2,—9 Geo. 3,	4		London,	1770	A.	J 6
Baluzius,	Capitularia Regum Francorum,	Fo.	2	Parisiis,	1780	A.	A 7
Bangor (Bishop of,)	Common Rights of Subjects,	8vo.	1	London,	1719	A.	A 7
Barbeyrac,	Histoire des Anciens Traités,	Folio.	2	Amsterdam, Haye,	1739	B.	A 6
"	Droit de la Guerre et de la Paix par Grotius,	4to.	2	Leyden,	1768	A.	A 3
"	Traité des Ambassadeurs,	4to.	1	Lallaye,	1723	B.	h
Barbier,	Dictionnaire des Ouvrages Anonymes,	8vo.	4	Paris,	1822—27	B.	I 7
Barlet,	Recueil d'Arrêts du Parlement de Paris,	Folio.	2	Avignon,	1773	A.	A 4
Barère,	La Liberté des Mers,	8vo.	2	Paris,	1798	A.	I 6
Barnabé le Vest,	Arrêts Célèbres du Parlement de Paris,	4to.	1	Paris,	1612	A.	P 6
Barnardiston,	Reports, K. B., 12 Geo. 1, (1714)—7 Geo. 2, (1734),	Folio.	2	In the Savoy,	1744	A.	O 5 & Q 6
Barnewall & Anderson,	" " 58 Geo. 2, (1817)—2 Geo. 4, (1821),	8vo.	4	London,	1818—21	A.	P
Barnewall & Cresswell,	" " 3 Geo. 4, (1822)—11 Geo. 4, (1830),	8vo.	10	"	1823—32	A.	P
Barnewall & Adolphus,	Reports K.B., 11 Geo. 4, (1830)—4 Wm. 4 (1834),	8vo.	5	London,	1831—35	B.	P
Bartolus,	Opera,	Folio.	11 in 6	Venetiis,	1615	A.	U 7
Basnage,	Œuvres,	Folio.	2	Rouen,	1709	A.	G 7
Basset,	Arrêts du Parlement de Dauphiné,	Folio.	1	Grenoble,	1676	B.	I 7
Battur,	Des Privilèges et Hypothèques,	8vo.	4	Paris,	1824	B.	E 5
Baudot,	Des Formalités Hypothécaires,	8vo.	2	"	1835	B.	E 5
Bayle—Mouillard,	De l'Emprisonnement pour Dettes,	8vo.	1	"	1836	B.	K 4
Beaubien,	Sur les-Loi Civiles du Bas-Canada,	8vo.	in 3	Montreal,	1832	A.	F 4
Beaussant,	Code Maritime,	8vo.	2	Paris,	1840	B.	J 2
Beawes,	Lex Mercatoria,	4to.	2	London,	1813	A.	J 6
Becca,	Des Délits et des Peines,	8vo.	1	Paris,	1822	A.	M 1
Beck,	Medical Jurisprudence,	8vo.	2	Albany,	1823	A.	M 3
Bedarride,	Du Dol et de la Fraude,	8vo.	3	Paris and Aix,	1852	B.	D 3
Bedel,	De l'Adultère,	8vo.	1	Paris,	1826	B.	C 2
Beijac,	Répertoire Général du Contentieux,	8vo.	2 in 1	Havre,	1850	B.	B 2
Belime,	Du Droit de Possession,	8vo.	1	Paris,	1842	B.	K 3
Bell,	Dictionary of Law of Scotland,	8vo.	1	Edinburgh,	1826	A.	K 3
Bellami,	Des Papiers Terriers,	4to.	1	Paris,	1746	A.	c l
Bellot,	Procédure Civile,	8vo.	1	Paris and Génève,	1837	A.	D 5
Benech,	Quotité disponible entre époux,	8vo.	1	Toulouse,	1841	B.	K 5
"	De l'Emploi et du Remploi de la Dot,	8vo.	1	Paris,	1847	B.	C 4

Author	Title	Size	No.	Place	Date		Mark
Bennett & Smith,	English Law and Equity Reports,	8vo.	26	Boston,	1851—55	A.	Q R 5
Bentham,	Œuvres de,	4to.	3	Bruxelles,	1840	B.	A 5
Berault, Godefroy & Airron,	Sur la Coutume de Normandie,	Folio.	2	Rouen,	1776	B.	C 7
Bérenger,	Novelles de Justinien,	4to.	2	Metz,	1811	B.	U 6
Berger,	De la Contribution à la Légitime,	18mo.	1	Paris,	1702	A.	D 4
Bergier,	Sur le Mariage des Protestans en 1785,	8vo.	1	Paris,	1787	B.	B 8
Bernardi,	Origine et Progrès de la Législation Française,	8vo.	1	Paris,	1816	B.	B 3
Berriot—St. Prix,	Procédure Civil,	8vo.	2	Paris,	1825	B.	K 5
"	Code Civile,	8vo.	3	"	1845—8	B.	G 4
Berryer,	Souvenirs de	8vo.	2 in 1	"	1839	A.	H 1
Berroyer & DeLauriere,	Bibliothèque des Coutumes,	4to.	1	"	1699	B.	B 6
"		4to.	1	"	1745	B.	
Bertauld,	De l'Hypothèque Légale des Femmes Mariées,	8vo.	1	"	1852	B.	E 5
Berthelot du Ferrier,	Cours de Code Pénal,	8vo.	1	Paris et Caen,	1854	B.	B 6
Berthelot,	Des Droits et Domaines du Roy,	4to.	1	Paris,	1719	B.	C 1
"	Des Éviction et la Garantie Formelle,	18mo.	2	"	1781	A.	C 1
Berthon,	Décisions du Droit Civil,	18mo.	1	Lyon,	1740	B.	h 4
Bescherelle,	Dictionnaire National,	Folio.	2	Paris,	1853	B.	L 5
Best,	On Presumptions,	4to.	1	London,	1844	B.	L 3
"	Right to begin and reply,	8vo.	1	"	1837	B.	t 1
Beugnot,	Assises de Jérusalem,	8vo.	2	Paris,	1841	B.	E 2
"	Les Olim, ou Registres des Arrêts, 1254-1318	Folio.	2	"	1842	B.	H 6
"	Parallèle du Code Pénal d'Angleterre, avec les lois Pénales Françoises,	4to.	4	"	1839—48	B.	
Bexon,		8vo.	1	"			
Bibaud,	Logique Judiciaire,	12mo.	1	Montreal,	1800	B.	M 1
Bible,		4to.	1	Oxford,	1828	A.	K 3
Bible,		12mo.	1	Edinburgh,	1714	A.	R 6
Bilhard,	Des Référés en France,	8vo.	1	Toulouse, Paris,	1834	A.	c 1
"	Bénéfice d'Inventaire,	8vo.	1	Paris,	1838	B.	K 3
Bingham,	Reports, C. P. 3 Geo. 4, (1822,)—4 Wm. 4, (1834),	8vo.	10	London,	1824—34	A.	D 4
"	New Cases, C. P. 4 Wm. 4, (1834,)—4 Vic., (1840),	8vo.	6	"	1835—41	A.	N 3
"	Reports, C. P. 2 Vic., (1839),	8vo.	pt. 3 of 5			A.	N 4
Bioche,	Dictionnaire de Procédure Civile et Commerciale,	8vo.	6	Paris,	1850—52	B.	K 5
"	Dictionnaire des Juges de Paix,	8vo.	2	"	1851—52	B.	K 4
Bisset,	On Partnership,	8vo.	1	Harrisburg,	1847	B.	J 5
Blackburn,	On Contract of Sale,	8vo.	1	London,	1845	A.	P 7
Blackstone, Sir W.,	Reports, K. B. and C. P., 20 Geo. 2, (1746,)—20 Geo. 3, (1779),	Folio.	2 in 2	"	1781	A.	N 7
"	" 11 Geo. 3, (1770,)—20 Geo. 3, (1779),	Folio.		"	1781	A.	P 6
Blackstone, H.,	Reports, C. P. and Ex., 28 Geo. 3, (1788)—36 Geo. 3, (1796),	8vo.	3	London,	1791—96	A.	s
Blackstone, Sir W.,	Commentaries,	8vo.	4	"	1809	A.	B 1
"	Commentaries sur les lois Anglaises,	8vo.	6	Paris,	1822—23	A.	D 3
Blackwell,	On Tax Titles,	8vo.	1	Chicago,	1855	B.	D 2
Flaize,	Des Monts de Piété,	8vo.	1	Paris,	1843	B.	o
Blanc,	De la Contrefaçon,	8vo.	1	"	1838	B.	Q 1
Blanchard,	Les Presidents au Mortier du Parlement de Paris,	Folio.	1	"	1647	B.	
Blatchford and Howlands,	Admiralty Reports,	8vo.	1	New York,	1855	A.	

Author.	Subject.	Size.	No. of Vols.	Where Published.	When.	Library.	Shelf.
Blaxland,	Codex Legum Anglicanarum,	8vo.	1	London,	1839	B.	a
Blondeau,	Du Bénéfice d'Inventaire,	8vo.	1	Paris,	1838	B.	U 4
"	Institutes de Justinien,	8vo.	2	"	1839	B.	U 4
"	Chrestomathie,	8vo.	1	"	1843	B.	A 3
Blondeau & Gueret,	Essais sur Législation ou Jurisprudence,	8vo.	1	"	1850	A.	J 7
Babé,	Journal du Palais,	Folio.	2	"	1755	B.	C 6
"	Coutumes de Meaux,	4to.	1	"	1683	B.	E 7
Bodin,	Les 6 livres de la République,	Folio.	1	London,	1577	A.	h
Bohn,	Catalogue,	8vo.	1	"	1848	A.	L 3
Bohun,	Institutio Legalis,	8vo.	1	In the Savoy,	1732	A.	G 4
Boileux,	Code Napoléon,	8vo.	2	Paris,	1852	B.	U 3
Bonjean,	Des Actions,	8vo.	2	"	1845	B.	M 2
Bonneville,	Du Régime Pénitentaire,	8vo.	1	"	1847	B.	K 4
Bonnier,	Des Preuves,	8vo.	1	"	1852	B.	C 1
Bordeaux,	Législation des Cours d'Eau,	8vo.	2	"	1849	A.	L 6
Bornier,	Conférence des Ordonnances de Louis XIV,	4to.	1	"	1744	A.	U 1
Bos,	Ellipses Graecae,	12mo.	1	Lugduni Batavorum,	1750	A.	H 7
Berthon,	Décisions du droit Civil, Canonique, &c.,	Folio.	1	Lyon,	1740	B.	N 2
Bosanquet et Puller,	Reports, C.P. and Ex. and H. of Lords, 36 Geo. 3, (1796).—44 Geo. 3, (1804),	8vo.	3	London,	1826	A.	N 3
"	New Reports, C. P., &c., 44 Geo. 3, (1804).—47 Geo. 3, (1807),	8vo.	2	"	1826	A.	B 6
Bosquet,	Dictionnaire raisonné des Domaines,	4to.	3	Rouen,	1762	A.	H 3
Bossuet,	Oraisons Funèbres,	18mo.	1	Paris,		B.	K 5
Boncenne,	Procédure Civile,	8vo.	6	"	1837—47	A.	U 6
Bouchaud,	Sur la loi des XII Tables,	4to.	2	"	1803	A.	K 7
Bouchel,	Bibliothèque, ou Trésor du Droit Français,	Folio.	3	"	1629	A.	J 6
"	Institutions Commerciales,	4to.	2	"	1801	B.	J 2
Boucher d'Argis,	Consulat de la Mer,	8vo.	2	"	1808	B.	C
"	Code Rural,	12mo.	1	Lyon,	1762	A.	K 2
"	De la Crne des Meubles,	18mo.	1	Paris,	1768	B.	C 4
"	Des Gains Nuptiaux,	4to.	2	"	1738	B.	B 5
Boucheul,	Institution au droit français,	12mo.	2	"	1771	B.	C 7
"	Coutume de Poitou,	Folio.	1	Poitiers,	1727	B.	D 5
Bonghier,	Des Conventions de succéder,	4to.	1	Paris,	1629	A.	H 6
Bouhier,	Arrêts de la Cour, &c.,	Folio.	3	Dijon,		B.	F 7
"	Œuvres de Jurisprudence,	L.8vo.	2	"	1787—89	B.	A 2
Bouillet,	Dictionnaire Universel d'Histoire et de Géographie,	12mo.	1	Paris,	1854	B.	J 3
Boutainvilliers,	Lettres sur les Anciens Parlemens,	8vo.	3	Londres,	1753	A.	J 5
Boulay Paty,	Droit Commercial Maritime,	4to.	4	Rennes,	1821—23	B.	J 2
"	Des Assurances,	8vo.	2	"	1827	A.	
"	Droit Commercial Maritime,	4to.	4	Paris,	1834	B.	
"	Des Faillites,	8vo.	2	"	1849	B.	

B

AUTHOR.	SUBJECT.	SIZE.	No. OF VOLS.	WHERE PUBLISHED.	WHEN.	LIBRARY.	SHELF.
Burge,	On Suretyship,	8vo.	1	London,	1849	B.	A 3
Buridan,	Coutumier de Vermandois,	Folio,	2	Paris,	1728	B.	C 7
Burke,	Contumes de Rheims,	Folio,	1	"	1665	B.	C 7
"	Lettres de	8vo.	3	"		B.	A 5
"	On Criminal Law,	12mo.	1	London,	1845	B.	M 2
"	Celebrated Trials, (Aristocracy),	8vo.	1	"	1849	B.	M 4
"	" (Upper Classes),	8vo.	1		1851		
Burrill,	On Circumstantial Evidence,	8vo.	1	New York,	1856	A.	M 3
Burlamaqui,	Principes du Droit, de la Nature et des Gens,	8vo.	in 5	Paris,	1820—21	A.	A 5
Burn,	Justice of the Peace,	8vo.	in 5	London,	1810	B.	M 1
"	Justice of the Peace,	8vo.	in 4	"	1788	A.	M 1
"	Law Dictionary,	8vo.	2	"	1792	A.	g
"	On Ecclesiastical Law,	8vo.	4	"	1824	A.	B 4
Burrow, Sir J	Reports, K. B., 30 Geo. 2, (1756)—12 Geo. 3, (1772),	8vo.	in 5	"	1790	A.	O 3
Brynkershock,	Du Juge Compétent des Ambassadeurs,	4to.	1	La Haye,	1723	A.	A 3
Butler, see							

Author.	Subject.	Size.	No. of Vols.	Where Published.	When.	Library.	Shelf.
Cadres,	Code Civil,	8vo,	1	Paris,	1845	R.	j 4
"	Des Enfants Naturels,	8vo,	1	"	1846	B.	D 4
Calmiel,	De la Folie,	8vo,	2	Paris,	1845	B.	M 2
Campbell,	Reports at N. P., K. B., and C. P., 43 Geo. 3; (1807)—56 Geo. 3; (1816),	8vo,	4	London,	1808—16	A.	P 4
"	Reports, N. P., 54 Geo. 3; (1814)—56 Geo. 3; (1816),	8vo,	1	"	1816	A.	P 4
"	Libel Act, see Parry.						
Camus,	Code Matrimonial,	4to,	2 in 1	Paris,	1770	B.	C 4
Canada,	Ordinances of Governor and Council of Province of Quebec,	Folio,	1	Quebec,	1762	A.	c
"	Edits. et Ordonnances,	4to,	2 1	"	1803—6	A.	
"	"	8vo,	1	"	1854	B.	d
"	P. Statutes, 1841, 5 Vic., 16 Vic., 1853,	{ 4to, 8vo,	{ 5 5 1 }	Montreal and Quebec,	1841—53	B.	d
"	Statuts	4to 8vo	12	Montreal, Queb. & Tor.	1841—53	A.	d
"	P. Statutes, 7 Vic., (1843)—20 Vic., 1857,	Folio,	3	Kingston & Montreal,	1843—57	A.	k
"	Journals of Legislative Council,	Folio,	5	"	1842—6	A.	j 1
"	Legislative Council Sessional Papers, 1842—6,	Folio,	8th		1843—6	A.	j 1
"	Journal of Legislative Assembly, 1849,	Folio,	2nd		1849	A.	j 1
"	Appendix to "	Folio,	1		1849	A.	j 1
"	Appendice,		2 1		1849	A.	j 1
"	Trade and Navigation Tables, 1850 and 1855,	8vo,	2 1	Toronto,	1851—6	A.	J 4
"	" in French,	8vo,	1	"	1851	A.	
"	Censuses,	8vo,		Quebec,	1853	A.	h 1
"	Badgley's Criminal Consolidation Act,	8vo,	1		1850	A.	
"	Gazette,	8vo,	12	Montreal and Quebec,	1850—55	A.	k
Canada, Lower,	Alien Act, 35 Geo. 3,	S. 4to,	1	Quebec,	1794	A.	i
"	Journals of House of Assembly, 32 Geo. 3; 1792—1813 53 Geo. 3;	4to,	12	"	1793—1813	A.	j 1
"	" " 44 Geo. 3; (1804)—54 Geo. 3; (1814),	4to,	8	"	1804—14	A.	j 1
"	" " (1810)—59 Geo. 3,	S. 4to,	11	"	1810	A.	j 1
"	" " 59 Geo. 3; (1819)—6 Wm. 4, (1826),	Folio,	3	"	1819—36	A.	j 1
"	Appendix to "	Folio,		"		A.	j 1
"	Appendix to 25th Vol of "	4to,	1	"	1817	A.	j 1
"	Journals Legislative Council, 35 Geo. 3; (1795)—; Wm. 4, (1836),	Folio,	20	"	1795—1836	A.	j
"	Provincial Statutes, 37 Geo. 3; (1797)—4 Wm. 4, (1833),	Folio,	10	"	1797—1833	A.	d 1
"	Index to Ordinances and Statutes to 57 Geo. 3,	4to,	11 & 12	"	1821—25	A.	d 1
"	Continuation of Index 7 Geo. 4,—2 Wm. 4,	8vo,	1	"	1817	A.	c
"	Revised Statutes,	8vo,	1	"	1832	B.	c
"	Statuts Revisés,	8vo,	1	Montreal,	1845	B.	d

Canada, Lower, ...	Reports, ... } See Lelievre,						
" " ...	Seignorial Court Reports, }						
Canada, Upper, ...	K. B. Reports, see Taylor,						
Capmas, ...	De la Révocation des Actes en Fraude de Creanciers, ...	Paris,	1	8vo.	1847	B.	D 2
Cardon, ...	Formulaire Général. ...	Paris,	2 in 1	8vo.	1817	A.	K 3
Caroccius, ...	Tractatus de Remediis, ...	Geneva,	1	8vo.	1521	A.	U 5
" ...	Tractatus de Juramenti Litis Decisorio, ...	Osnaburgi,	1	S. 4to	1676	A.	U 5
Carpentier, ...	Glossarium Novum ad Scriptores Medii Ævi, ...	Paris,	4	Folio.	1766	B.	T 7
Carré, ...	Du Gouvernement des Paroisses, ...	Paris,	1	8vo.	1839	B.	B 3
Carre & Chauveau, ...	Procedure Civile, ...	"	in 7	8vo.	1843	B.	K 5
" " ...	" ...	"	1	8vo.	1853	B.	K 4
Carrey, ...	Actes du Gouvernement Provisoire, 1848, ...	Paris,	1	12mo.	1848	B.	G
Carrington & Payne, ...	Reports at N. P., 7 Geo. 4, (1827)—4 Vic. (1841), K. B. and C. P., ...	London,	in 9	8vo.	1829—41	A.	P 4
Carrington & Marshman, ...	Reports at N. P., 4 Vic., (1841)—6 Vic. (1843), Q. B., C. P. & Ex., ...	"	1	8vo.	1843	A.	P 4
Carrington & Kirwan, ...	Reports at N. P., 6 Vic., (1843)—13 Vic. (1850), Q. B., C. P. & Ex., ...	"	2	8vo.	1845—50	A.	P 4
Caseneuve, ...	Le Franc Alen de la Provence de Languedoc, ...	Toulouse,	1	Folio.	1645	B.	D 7
Cassan, ...	Le Nouveau et Parfait Notaire, ...	Paris,	1	4to.	1749	A.	L 6
Cauchy, ...	Du Duel, ...	"	2 in 1	8vo.	1846	B.	M 2
Cellier, ...	Cours de Redaction Notariale, ...	Paris,	1	8vo.	1840	B.	K 3
Chabot, ...	Dictionnaire des Connaissances Elementaires, ...	"	1	8vo.	1854	B.	A 3
Chabot, ...	Questions Transitoires sur le Code Civil, ...	Dijon,	3	8vo.	1829	A.	G 4
Chabot (de l'Allier), ...	" Napoléon, ...	Paris,	2	4to.	1809	A.	G 4
" ...	" Civil, ...	Dijon,	3	8vo.	1829	B.	G 4
" ...	Des Successions, ...	Paris,	3	8vo.	1832	A.	D 4
" ...	Des Successions, ...	Dijon et Paris,	3	8vo.	1839	B,	D 4
Chaillaud, ...	Dictionnaire des Eaux et Forêts, ...	Paris,	2	4to.	1769	A.	D 5
Chaline, ...	Méthode Générale pour l'Intelligence des Coutumes de France, ...	Metz,	1	S. 4to.	1725	B.	E 3
Chalmers, ...	Treaties, ...	London,	2	8vo.	1790	B.	A 1
Championnière, ...	Droits d'Enregistrement, ...	Paris,	5	8vo.	1839—41	B.	B 1
" ...	Supplement to do, ...	"	1	8vo.	1851	B.	B 1
" ...	De la Propriété des Eaux Courantes, ...	"	1	8vo.	1846	B.	C 1
Chambers & Peterson, ...	Law of Railway Companies, ...	London,	1	8vo.	1848	B.	D 2
Chambers, ...	Law of Elections, ...	"	1	8vo.	1837	A.	A
Charlton, ...	Du Dol, ...	Avallon,	3	8vo.	1828	A.	D 3
" ...	De Droit d'Alluvion, ...	Paris,	1	8vo.	1840	B.	C 1

Author.	Subject.	Size.	No. of Vols.	Where Published.	When.	Library.	Shelf.
Charles—Chabot,	Dictionnaire des Connaissances Municipales,	8vo.	1	Paris,	1854	B.	
Charondas,	Responses du Droit Français,	8vo.	1	Lyon,	1600	B.	E 6
Chassan,	Des Delits et Contravention de la Parole,	8vo.	2 in 1	Paris,	1846	B.	M 2
Chavot,	De la Propriété Mobilière,	8vo.		Paris, Lyon,	1839	B.	C 3
Chitty,	On Bills,	8vo.	1	Springfield,	1849	B.	J 2
"	On Bills,	8vo.	1	London,	1812	A.	J 4
"	On Criminal Law,	8vo.	in 4	"	1816	A.	M 5
"	"	8vo.	in 4	"	1816	A.	M 5
"	"	8vo.	in 4	"	1816	A.	
"	On Commercial Law,	8vo.	in 4	"	1826	A.	
"	On Descents,	8vo.	1	"	1824	A.	J 4
Chitty & Hulme,	Statutes of Practical Utility, 9 Henry 3,—9 Geo. 4,	8vo.	2	"	1825	A.	D 3
Chitty,	" " 13 Edward 1,—1 Vic.,	8vo.	2	"	1828	A.	c 1
Chitty, Jr.	General Practice,	8vo.	4	"	1837	A.	c 1
	On Office of Constable,	12mo.	1	Philadelphia,	1836—9	B.	
Chopin,	Sur la Coutume d'Anjou,			London,		B.	M 2
Cicero,	Opera,	Folio.	5	Paris,	1662	B.	F 7
Cigne?,	De la Propriété,	Folio.	4 in 2	Colonie Allobrogum,	1616	A.	U 1
Clair et Clapier,	Barreau Anglais,	8vo.	1	Guingamp,	1839	B.	H 1
Cleirac,	Us et Coutumes de la Mer,	8vo.	3	Paris,	1824	B.	J 6
Clercq, (Le.)	Droit Romain,	4to.	1	Rouen,	1671	B.	U 4
Clift,	New Book of Declarations, &c.,	8vo.	8	Liège,	1810—12	A.	L 7
Cobbett,	Parliamentary History of England, 1066—1803,	Folio.	1	London,	1719	A.	o p q
Cochin,	Œuvres,	8vo.	36	London,	1806—20	A.	H 3
Coderre,	Procès d'Anais Toussaint,	8vo.	8	Paris,	1788	A.	M 3
Coffinières,	De la Liberté Individuelle,	8vo.	1	Montreal,	1857	B.	B 5
Coin, Delisle,	Commentaire Analytique du Code Civil,	8vo.	2	Paris,	1840	B.	G 5
"	Limite du Droit de Rétention par l'Enfant Donataire Renonçant,	4to.	1	Paris,	1846	B.	D 4
		8vo.	1	"	1852	B.	

Author	Title	Vols.	Size	Place	Date	Class	Shelf
Coke, Sir E.,	Reports, K. B., &c., 14 Eliz., (1572)—13 Jas. 1, (1616),	7	8vo.	In the Savoy,	1738	A.	O 3
Coke,	Upon Littleton,	2	8vo.		1832	A.	D 6
Cole,	On Quo Warranto,	1	12mo.	London,	1843	B.	R 1
Coleman & Caines,	Reports Sup. Court, N. Y., 1794—1805,	1	8vo.	New York,	1808	A.	M 4
Collard,	Des Circonstances Atténuantes,	1	8vo.	Paris, Nancy,	1840	B.	C 1
Collier,	On Mines,	1	12mo.	London,	1849	B.	J 3
Collyer,	On Partnership,	1	8vo.	Springfield,	1834	B.	O 6
Comberbach,	Reports K. B., 1 James 2, (1685)—10 Wm. 3, (1698),	1	Folio.	In the Savoy,		A.	B 2
Commission du Clergé,	Memoires du Clergé de France dans l'Affaire des Foi et Hommages,	1	8vo.	Amsterdam,	1785	B.	C 3
Comte,	De la Propriété,	2	8vo.	Paris,	1834	B.	J 5 a
Comyn,	On Contracts,	2	8vo.	London,	1807	A.	
"	Digest of Laws of England,	1	8vo.	"	1822	A.	
Coode,	On Legislative Expression,	1	8vo.	London,	1852	B.	G 7
Coquille,	Œuvres,	2	Folio.	Paris,	1665	A.	E 5
Corail de Saint Foy,	Questions sur l'Edit de Juin, 1771,	1	8vo.	Toulouse,	1785	B.	E 6
Cor ,	Code de Henri IV.,	1	8vo.	Rouen,	1615	B.	C
Corvinus,	Jus Feudale,	1	8vo.	Dublin,	1762	A.	G 4
Cotelli,	Cours de Droit Français,	2	8vo.	Paris,	1814	A.	K 2
Couchot,	Le Practicien Universel,	6	12mo.	Paris,	1725—38	A.	Q 3
Cowen,	Reports, Superior Court, N. Y., 1829,	in 9	8vo.	Albany,	1835—9	A.	
Cowen & Hill,	Notes to Phillips on Evidence,	in 2	8vo.	New York,	1843	A.	
Cowper,	Reports, K. B., 14 Geo. 3, (1774)—18 Geo. 3, (1778),	1	8vo.	Dublin,	1794	A.	O 3
"	"	in 2	8vo.	London,	1800	A.	O 3
Cox,	Criminal Law Cases,	6	8vo.	London,	1846	A.	M 4
Craig,	Political Science,	3	8vo.	Edinburgh,	1814	A.	A 3
Cranch,	Reports, Supreme Court U. S., 1801—1814,	8	8vo.	Washington,	1804—16	A.	
Cripps,	Church and Clergy Law,	1	8vo.	London,	1850	B.	Q

Author.	Subject.	Size.	No. of Vols.	Where Published.	When.	Library.	Shelf.
Croke, Sir G.,	Reports, K. B. and C. B., 1 Car. 1, (1625)—16 Car. 1, (1641),	Folio.	1	London,	1657	A.	O 6
"	Reports, "	Folio.	1	"	1683	A.	O 6
"	Reports, K. B. and C. B., 24 Eliz., (1582)—45 Eliz., (1603),	Folio.	1	"	1683	A.	O 6
"	Reports, K. B., 1 Jas.,	Folio.	1	"	1683	B.	O 6
Cross,	On Lien,	8vo.	1	London,	1840	B.	J 2
Cruise,	Digest of Laws of England,	8vo.	6	London,	1824	A.	E 6
Culain,	Des Droits des Femmes,	8vo.	1	Paris,	1842	B.	C 4
Cumberland,	Des Loix Naturelles,	4to.	1	Amsterdam,	1744	A.	A 6
Cujacius,	Opera Omnia,	Folio.	3	Lutetiæ Parisiorum,	1658	A.	S 7
"	Appendix to do.,	Folio.	1				S 7
Curasson,	Opera Postuma,	Folio.	6	Lutetiæ Parisiorum,	1658	A.	S T 7
"	Des Actions Possessoires,	8vo.	1	Dijon,	1842	B.	K 3
Curtiss,	Report of Case and Judgment in Martin vs. Escot,	8vo.	1	London,	1841	B.	B 3

Author	Subject	No. of Vols.	Size	Where Published	When	Library	Shelf
D'Aguesseau,	Œuvres,						
Dallas,	Questions sur les Substitutions,	13	4to.	Paris,	1759—89	A.	F 6
Dalloz,	Pennsylvania Reports, 1790—1806,	1	4to.	Toulouse,	1770	B.	E 4
Dalloz,	Journal des Audiences,	4	8vo.	Philadelphia,	1806—7	A.	R 1
Dalloz & Tourneminc,	Journal des Audiences,	12	4to.	Paris,	1824—30	A.	H & 15
"	Jurisprudence Generale du Royaume, 1825—37,	27	4to.	"	1822—4	A.	13
Damonrs,	Conference de l'Ordonnance des Donations, avec le Droit Romain,	2	4to.	Paris,	1825—52	B.	H & 15
Danson & Lloyd,	Reports, Mercantile Cases, 1822 and 1829,	1	8vo.	Paris,	1753	B.	E 4
Dantoine,	Regles du Droit Civil,	1	8vo.	London,	1830	A.	P 4
Danty,	De la Preuve,	1	4to.	Brussels,	1742	B.	U 5
"	De la Preuve,	1	4to.	Paris,	1697	A.	K 6
Danvers,	Abridgment of Common Law,	1	4to.	Paris,	1753	A.	L 6
Daour,	Imlex Juris Civilis,	2	Folio.	London,	1705—13	A.	O 7
D'Arbelles,	Memoire sur le Conduite de la France et de l'Angleterre a l'egard des Neutres,	1	Folio.	Lugduni,	1612	B.	R 7
Darca,	Des Injures,	1	8vo.	Paris,	1810	B.	A 5
D'Argentré,	Commentaria in Patrias Britonum Leges,	1	18mo.	Paris,	1775	A.	F 7
Davie,	Cours d'Eau,	1	Folio.	Paris,	1621	B.	C 1
Davis,	Quaker Law,	3	8vo.	Paris,	1845	B.	B 3
Davison & Merivale,	Reports, Q.B. and Ex., 6 Vic., (1843)—7 Vic., (1844),	1	8vo.	Bristol,	1820	A.	P 3
Davol,	Du Droit Français, Bourgoyne,	1	12mo.	London,	1844	B.	E 2
Deacon,	Digest of Criminal Law,	in	8vo.	Dijon,	1757—67	A.	M 4
Deacon & Chitty,	Reports, Bankruptcy, 5 Wm. 4, (1835)—3 Vic., (1840),	2	8vo.	London,	1831	A.	N 1
Dearsly,	Reports, Bankruptcy, 2 Wm. 4, (1832)—5 Wm. 4, (1835),	4	8vo.	"	1837—41	A.	N & N 1
DeBeaufort,	On Criminal Process,	1	12mo.	"	1833—7	B.	M 2
DeBeaumont,	Recueil Concernant le Tribunal des Marechaux de France,	1	8vo.	London,	1853	B.	K 2
DeBeaumont & DeTocqueville,	Jurisprudence des Rentes,	2	12mo.	Paris,	1784	B.	C 2
DeBlegny,	Système Penitentiaire aux Etats Unis,	1	12mo.	Paris,	1784	B.	M 2
DeBonne,	Manière de Vérifier les Écritures Contestées en Justice,	1	12mo.	"	1845	B.	K 2
DeBrésoles,	Precis of Militia Act, 34 Geo. 3,	1	S. 4to.	Quebec,	1698	A.	c 1
DeBua,	Pratique des Officialités,	4 in 2	4to.	Quebec,	1781	B.	B 5
DeBurilan,	Les Origines,	3	8vo.	Paris et Dijon,	1789	A.	A 2
DeCabanel,	Contume de Rheims,	1	Folio.	LaHaye,	1665	B.	C 7
DeCambolas,	Coutumier de Vermandois,	1	8vo.	Paris,	1728	B.	C 7
DeCastellan,	Décisions Notables,	1	12mo.	"	1749	B.	C 2
DeCerfrol,	Maximes Générales sur les Droits Domaniaux,	1	4to.	Toulouse,	1744	B.	H 6
DeChampeaux,	Arrêta du Parlement de Toulouse,	1	4to.	Toulouse,	1744	B.	I 6
DeCharlevoix,	Legislation du Divorce,	1	S. 8vo.	Londres,	1723	B.	C 2
DeCormis,	Droit Civil Ecclesiastique,	in 6	8vo.	Paris,	1769	B.	B 4
	Histoire de la Nouvelle France,	3	18mo.	Paris,	1744	B.	T 2
	...eil de Consultations,	2	Folio.	Paris,	1735	A.	H 7

Author	Title	Size	Vols	Place	Year		
DeCussy,	Dictionnaire du Diplomate,	12mo.	1	Leipzig,	1846	B.	A 3
DeFelice,	Droit de la Nature et des Gens,	8vo.	2 in 2	Paris,	1830	B.	A 5
DeGama,	Sur le Droit d'Aubaine,	18mo.	2 in 1	Paris,	1706	B.	B 4
DeGarden,	De Diplomatie,	8vo.	3	Paris,	1833	B.	A 3
	Histoire des Traités de Paix,	8vo.	13	Paris,		B.	A 1
DeGerando,	Institutes du Droit Administratif Français,	8vo.	4	Paris,	1829—30	A.	B 4
DeGourcy,	L'Etat des Personnes en France sous la 1e et 2e race de nos Rois,	18mo.	1	Paris,	1769	B.	B 4
DeGrainville,	Recueil d'Arrêts,	4to.	1	Paris,	1750	A.	H 6
"	"	4to.	1	Paris,	1750	B.	H 6
DeGravina,	Histoire de la Legislation chez les Romains,	4to.	1	Paris,	1758	A.	H 6
DeGueidan,	Discours prononcés au Parlement de Provence,	8vo.	3	Paris,	1829	A.	U 4
DeHericourt,	De la Vente des Immeubles par Decret,	18mo.	2 in 1	Paris,	1739—45	A.	I 2
"	Loix Ecclesiastiques de la France,	4to.		Paris,	1752	A.	K 6
"	Œuvres Posthumes,	Folio.	4	"	1756	A.	A 7
"	Loix Ecclesiastiques,	4to.	4	"	1759	A.	G 6
DeJouy,	Conférences des Ordonnances,	Folio.	1	"	1759	A.	G 6
De la Borde,	Des Avaries Particulières,	4to.	1	Paris,	1771	A.	A 7
De la Champagne,	De la Legitime, Representation et Secondes Noces,	8vo.	1	Paris,	1753	A.	L 6
De la Combe,	Recueil de Jurisprudence Civile,	18mo.	1	Paris,	1838	B.	J 5
"	Commentaire sur les Nouvelles Ordonnances,	4to.	1	Paris,	1720	B.	D 3
"	Recueil de Jurisprudence Canonique,	4to.	1	Paris,	1746	A.	e
"	Recueil de Jurisprudence Civile,	Folio.	1	Paris,	1753	A.	E 4
De la Mothe,	Œuvres de M. Ant. D'Espeisses; see D'Espeisses,	4to.	1	Paris,	1771	A.	H 7
			1		1761	A.	e
De la Croix,	Constitutions des Principaux Etats,	8vo.	6	Paris,	1791	B.	A 2
De la Garde,	Souveraineté du Roy,	4to.	2		1767	B.	B 6
Delalande,	Coutume d'Orleans,	Folio.	2	Orleans,	1704—5	C.	C 7
Delamare,	De la Police,	Folio.	4	Paris,	1705—33	A.	A 7
Delamare et Poitvin,	Du Contrat de Commission,	8vo.	4	Paris,	1840—7	B.	J 2
De la Marsonnière,	Contrainte par Corps; see Marsonnière,						
De la Mothe,	Essais de Jurisprudence,	18mo.	5	Paris,	1757	A.	B 1
De la Montre,	Questions de Droit,	12mo.	1	"	1770	B.	E 2
DeLanglade,	Du Pret sur Hypothèque,	8vo.	1	Paris,	1847	B.	E 5
DeLanglé,	Conférence du Code Civil,	8vo.	8	Paris,	1805	G.	G 2
De la Porte et Caubray,	Des Sociétés Commerciales,	8vo.	2 in 1	Paris,	1843	J.	J 3
De la Porte,	Les Pandectes Françaises,	8vo.	15	Paris,	1803—6	F.	F 2
De la Roche-Flavien,	Discussion du Code Civil; see Jonanneau,						
De la Rouvière,	Arrêts Notables du Parlement de Toulouse,	4to.	1	Toulouse,	1693	B.	I 6
De la Serra,	De la Revocation et Nullité des Donations,	4to.	1	Toulouse,	1738	A.	E 4
De la Thaumassière,	Contrat du Change; see Dupuy de la Serra,						
De la Touloubre,	Coutume de Berri,	Folio.	1	Bourges,	1701	E.	B 7
DeLaurière,	Jurisprudence Féodale de la Provence et du Languedoc,	8vo.	2	Avignon,	1765	E.	C
"	Des Institutions et Substitutions,	12mo.	2	Paris,	1715	B.	D 3
"	Institutes de Loisel,	12mo.	2	"	1715	B.	D 3
"	Coutume de Paris,	18mo.	2	"	1783	A.	E 3
"	Institutes Coutumières de Loisel,	12mo.	2	"	1777	B.	E 3
"	Ordonnances des Roys de France, Capet, 1473,	18mo.	in 2	"	1783	A.	E 3
		Folio.	17	"	1723—1820		r 5

Author	Subject	Size	No. of Vols.	Where Published	When	Library	Shelf
DeLaurière et al,	Table Générale des 9 1res vol. des Ordonnances: see DeVillevault.						
Delabreque,	Legislation des Mines, &c,	8vo.	2	Paris,	1838	B.	C 1
Delisle,	Interpretation Juridique,	8vo.	2	Paris,	1819	E.	A 5
Delourneau,	Maximes Générales du Droit Français,	12mo.	1	Rouen,	1616	H.	E 2
Delpan,	Histoire de l'Action Publique,	8vo.	2 in 1	Paris,	1830	H.	K 4
Delvincourt,	Cours de Code Civil,	4to.	3	Paris, Dijon,	1834	A.	G 5
"	Institutes de Droit Commercial,	8vo.	2 in 1	Paris,	1831	B.	J 3
DeMaleville,	Analyse Raisonnée de la Discussion du Code Civil,	8vo.	4	Paris,	1822	A.	G 2
DeMongeat,	Des Dépôts; see Aublet de Maubuy,						
DeHaluy,	De la Condition Civile des Étrangers en France,	8vo.	1	Paris,	1841	B.	B 4
DeAlmodier,	Histoire de Henry VII. d'Angleterre,	18mo.	2	Paris,	1799	A.	S 2
Decralomte,	Code Civil,	8vo.	1	Paris,	1845—53	H.	G 5
D'Monchobou,	De la Distinction des Biens,	8vo.	1	"	1854	B.	H 6
DeMontavilon,	Arrêts en Robes Rouges,	S. 4to.	1	Paris,	1629	E.	D 5
DeMoulin,	Des Successions,	4to.	2	Aix,	1786	A.	I 3
Demeviers,	Coutume de Paris; see Mr-villiens,						
Denisart,	Journal des Audiences, Cour de Cassation, 1791—1839,	4to.	18	Paris,	1809	A.	I 1
"	Collection de Décisions Nouvelles,	18mo.	6	Paris,	1754	A.	c 1
"	Actes de Notoriété,	4to.	1	"	1758	A.	e 1
"		4to.	4	"	1771	A.	e 1
"	Collection de Décisions Nouvelles,	4to.	4	"	1784	A.	e 1
Denis-au,	Collection de Décisions Nouvelles,	4to.	3rd	"	1788—1807	A.	c 1
DeFarlou,	Crown Cases, 1844—1850,	4to.	13	London,	1850	A.	er
DePousey,	Sur les Actions Possessoires,	8vo.	1	Paris,	1850	B.	M 4
Dedichelourre,	Traité des Fiefs; see Henrion de Pensey,						K 3
Dermisseau,	Nouveau Coutumier Général,	Folio.	8	Paris,	1724	A.	B 7
DeSalviat,	Traité de la Subrogation,	4to.	1	"	1713	A.	E 4
DeSavigny,	Jurisprudence du Parlement de Bordeaux,	4to.	2	Paris et Limoges,	1824	B.	G 6
Descogilet,	Droit Romain,	8vo.	8 in 4	Paris,	1840—50	B.	U 4
DesMaisous,	Les Loix des Bâtimens,	8vo.	1	Paris,	1776	B.	D 2
Desmarquets,	Nouveau Recueil d'Arrêts du Parlement de Paris,	Folio.	1	Paris,	1667	B.	I 7
"	Nouveau Stil du Châtelet de Paris,	4to.	1	Paris,	1746	E.	K 6
DeSerans,	Sur les Coutumes de Chasteau-Neuf, Chartres et Dreux,	4to.	1	Chartres,	1771	E.	K 6
D'Espeisses,	Œuvres,	S. 4to.	1	Lyon,	1645	B.	G 7
Desquiron,	De la Preuve par Témoins,	Folio.	3 in 1	Toulouse,	1726	A.	G 6
"	Du Domicile,	4to.	3	Paris,	1778	A.	K 4
"	De la Mort Civile,	8vo.	1	"	1811	A.	A 4
DeVillevault,	Table Générale des 9 vol. du Recueil des Ordonnances des Roys de France,	8vo.	1	"	1812	B.	M 2
		Folio.	1	Paris,	1757	A.	r

Author	Title	Place	Vols	Size	Date		Code
DeVilleneuve et Massé,	Dictionnaire du Contentieux Commercial,	Paris,	1	8vo.	1840	B.	J 6
DeVisme,	Science Parfaite des Notaires,	Paris,	2	4to.	1771	A.	L 6
D'Hoguive,	des Interets des Créances,	"	1	18mo.	1774	B.	D -
"	Coutumes de Boulonnois,	"	1	4to.	1777	B.	C 6
Dickinson,	Justice of the Peace,	London,	3	8vo.	1822	A.	M 1
Dillon,	Case of Children of Duke of Sussex,	London,	1	4to.	1832	B.	D 4
Doolson,	Reports, Admiralty, 1811–1822,	London,	2	8vo.	1815—28	A.	N
D'Olive,	Arrests du Parlament de Toulouse,	Toulouse,	1	4to.	1682	A.	H 6
Domat,	Loix Civiles,	Paris,	1	Folio.	1756	B.	E 7
"	Œuvres Complètes,	Paris,	2 in 1	8vo.	1828—29	B.	E 3
Domenget,	Institutes de Gaius,	"	1	8vo.	1841	B.	K 3
Dorgelles,	Traité élémentaire des Actions Privées,	Paris,	1	12mo.	1847	B.	U 4
Dorigny,	De l'Assistance Judiciaire,	Paris,	1	Folio.	1828	B.	U 7
	Opera Omnia,	Rome,	12 in 6	8vo.	1852	A.	O 3
Douglas,	Reports, K. B., 10 Geo. 3, (1759)—23 Geo.3, (1783),	London,	4	8vo.	1813 & 1831	A.	P 6
"	Reports, K. B., 19 Geo. 3, (1778)—21 Geo.3, (1780),	London,	1	8vo.	1786	A.	O 5
Dowling & Ryland,	Reports, K. B., 2 Geo. 4, (1822)—7 Geo. 4, (1827),	London,	8	8vo.	1822—7	B.	C 5
Dubost,	Jurisprudence du Conseil,	Paris,	3	4to.	1660	B.	C 5
Dubury,	De la Représentation des Filles,	Paris,	1	S. 4to.	1845	A.	M 4
DuBuys,	Histoire du Droit Criminel,					A.	
DuCange,	Glossarium: see DuFresne.						
DuCaurroy de la Croix,	Institutes de Justinien,	Paris,	2	8vo.	1822—3	B.	U 4
DuFresne,	Glossarium ad Scriptores Mediæ et Infimæ Latinitatis,	Paris,	6	Folio.	1733—6	A.	T 7
"	Journal des Audiences, 1622–1664,	Paris,	1	Folio.	1757	B.	J 7
"	De la Séparation des Patrimoines,	Paris et Orleans,	1	S. 4to.	1842	B.	C 4
DuL'rens,	Les Trois Coutumes,	Chartres,	1	8vo.	1845	B.	C 6
Dumont,	Organisation des Cours d'Eau,	Paris,	1	4to.	1845	A.	C 1
Dumoulin,	Des Fiefs,	Paris,	2	8vo.	1773	A.	C 5
Duncomb,	Trials per Pais,	London,	1	8vo.	1766	B.	L 2
Dunkin,	Address against Seignorial Bill of 1854,	Quebec,	1	4to.	1853	B.	C 6
Dunod,	Coutume de Bourgogne,	Besançon,	1	8vo.	1756	B.	C 4
"	De la Mainmorte,	Paris,	1	4to.	1760	A.	C 4
"	Des Prescriptions,	"	1	4to.	1810	B.	C 4
Dunod de Charnage,	Des Prescriptions,	"	1	4to.	1774	A.	C 4
Dupare (Poulain),	See Poulain du Parc,						
DuPerier,	Œuvres,	Avignon,	3	4to.	1759	A.	G 6
Dupin,	Coutume de Bordeaux,	Bordeaux,	1	Folio.	1737	B.	B 7
"	De Pénes des Secondes Noces,	Paris,	1	4to.	1743	A.	C 4
"	De l'Autorité Ecclésiastique,	"	3	18mo.	1768	B.	B 3
"	Profession d'Avocat,	"	2	8vo.	1832	A.	h
"	Jésus devant Caïphe et Pilate,	"	1	24mo.	1840	B.	M 2
"	Du Droit Public Ecclésiastique français,	"	1	18mo.	1845	B.	B 3
"	Constitution de la République Française,	"	1	12mo.	1849	B.	H 3
"	Requisitoires, Plaidoyers, &c.,	"	11	8vo.	1836—52	B.	
Duplessis,	Coutume de Paris,	Paris,	2	Folio.	1754	B.	F 7
"	Traités de	"	2	Folio.	1754	A.	F 7
Dupuy de la Serra,	Contrat de Change, (bound with Jousse.)	Poitiers,	1	8vo.	1828	B.	J 3

Author	Subject	Size	No. of Vols.	Where Published.	When.	Library.	Shelf.
Durand,	Institutes du Droit Canonique,	18mo.	9	Lyon,	1770	A.	B 2
"	De la Loi sur la Contrainte par Corps,	8vo.	1	Paris,	1851	B.	K 4
Durand de Maillane,	Dictionnaire de Droit Canonique,	4to.	4	Lyon,	1770	A.	B 5
Durand, Saint Amand,	Manuel des Courtiers de Commerce,	8vo.	1	Paris,	1845	B.	J 2
Duranton,	Cours de Droit Français,	8vo.	19	Paris,	1834—5	A.	P 5
Durnford & East,	Reports, K. B, 26 Geo. 3, (1785)—32 Geo. 3, (1791)	8vo.	4	Dublin,	1788—93	A.	O 6
"	Reports, K. B, 39 Geo. 3, (1798)—40 Geo. 3, (1800)	Folio.	in 8	London,	1800	A.	O 6
"	Term Reports, K. B, 27 Geo. 3, (1787)—40 Geo. 3, (1800),	8vo.	8	London,	1817	A.	O 4
Duvergier,	Collection des Lois, 1788—1852,	8vo.	39	Paris,	1834	A.	F G 1
"	Droit Civil Français,	8vo.	6	Paris,	1835—43	A.	G 4
Dwarris,	On Statutes,	8vo.	1	London,	1830	A.	L 2

Author.	Subject.	Size.	No. of Vols.	Where Published.	When.	Library.	Shelf.
Eardley, Wilmot,	On Burglary,	8vo.	1	London,	1851	B.	M 1
East,	Pleas of the Crown,	8vo.	2	{ 1st, London,.... / 2nd, Philadelphia, }	1803	A.	O 3 4
"	Reports, K. B., 41 Geo. 3, (1800)—53 Geo. 3, (1812)	8vo.	16	London,	1801—14	A.	K 3
Edwards,	Admiralty Jurisdiction,	8vo.	1	London,	1847	B.	B 3
Egan,	On Status of Jews in England,	8vo.	1	London,	1848	B.	I 7
Eimé,	Arrests Notables du Parlement de Provence,	Folio.	1	Paris,	1750	A.	J 2
Ellis,	Law of Debtor and Creditor,	8vo.	1	London,	1822	A.	J 5
"	On Fire and Life Insurance and Annuities,	8vo.	1	"	1832	A.	J 5
Emerigon,	Des Assurances et Contrats à la Grosse,	4to.	2	Marseilles,	1783	A.	B 3
"	On Insurances,	8vo.	1	London,	1850	B.	C 1
Engel,	Jus Canonicum,	12mo.	3	Vindobonæ,	1761	A.	Q 7
Erskine,	Principles of Law of Scotland,	8vo.	1	Edinburgh,	1809	A.	P 3
"	Institutes of Law of Scotland,	Folio.	2	Edinburgh,	1828		
Espinasse,	Reports at N. P., Q. B. & C. P., 33 Geo. 3, (1793)—47 Geo. 3, (1807)	8vo.	6 in 3	London.	1801—11		

Author	Subject	Size	No. of Vols.	Where Published.	When.	Library.	Shelf.
Faber,	Codex Fabrianus,	Folio.	1	Colonie Allobrogum,	1710	B.	R 7
Fabrott,	Justiniani Institutiones,	12mo.	1	Lugduni Batavorum,	1733	A.	U 5
Fauchet,	De la Religion Nationale, (Bound with Flassan)	8vo.	1	Paris,	1789	E.	C 2
Fearne,	On Contingent Remainders,	8vo.	1	London,	1831	A.	D 6
Feliens,	Ordonnances et Instructions, Charles 7,—Français,	S.Fol.	1	Paris,		A.	t
Fell,	Ou Mercantile Guarantees,	8vo.	1	London,	1820	A.	J 1
Fenet,	Recueil Complet des Travaux Preparatoires du Code Civil,	8vo.	15	Paris,	1827	A.	G 2
Ferand, Girand,	Servitudes de Voirie,	8vo.	2	Paris, Aix,	1850	B.	C 2
"	Législation des Chemins de Fer,	8vo.	2	"	1853	A.	D 2
Ferrière,	Grande Coutume de Paris,	Folio.	4	Paris,	1714	A.	D 7
"	Nouvelle Introduction à la Pratique,	4to.	in 2	"	1734	A.	e
"	Coutume de Paris,	18mo.	in 2	"	1762	A.	e
"	Dictionnaire de Droit et de Pratique,	4to.	in 7	"	1787—8	A.	U 3
"	Institutes de Justinien,	12mo.		Paris,		A.	B 6
Fessard,	Dictionnaire de l'Enregistrement,	4to.	2	Paris,	1844	A.	c 1
Fessenden,	Interest Tables,	8vo.	2 in 1	Montreal,	1822	A.	A 7
Fevret,	De l'Abus,	Folio.	1	Lyon,	1677	A.	N 6
Finch,	Reports, Chancery, 25 Car. 2, (1673)—32 Car. 2, (1680).	Folio.	1	In the Savoy,	1725	A.	b 1
Fish,	Exchequer Digest,	8vo.	1	Philadelphia,	1855	B.	M 3
Fitzherbert,	New Natura Brevium,	8vo.	1	Dublin.	1793	A.	C 2
Flandin,	Des Poisons,	8vo.	3	Paris,	1846—53	A.	A
Flassan,	La Question du Divorce,	S. 4to	1	Paris,	1790	A.	A
Fleta,	Commentarius Juris Anglicani,	8vo.	1	London,	1647	A.	M 3
Flintoff,	On Laws of England and Wales,	8vo.	6	London,	1840	B.	S 2
Foderé,	Medicine Légale,	8vo.	15	Paris,	1813	B.	A 4
Felix,	Revue Etrangère et Française de Legislation,	8vo.	1	Paris,	1834—48	B.	C 2
Felix et Henrion,	Du Droit International Privé,	8vo.	1	"	1852	A.	E 4
Fons,	Des Rentes Foncières,	12mo.	1	Paris,	1828	B.	K 6
Foutanon,	Aphorismes de Droit,	4to.	1	Paris,	1846	B.	Q 7
"	La Pratique de Masuer,	Folio.	1	In the Savoy,	1681	A.	P 6
Fortescue, Sir J.,	De Laudibus Legum Angliæ,	Folio.	1	In the Savoy,	1741	B.	M 3
Fortescue, Lord,	Reports, Exc., K. B., 10 An., (1712)—9 Geo. 1, (1714)	8vo.	1	London,	1748	B.	D 7
Forsyth,	History of Trial by Jury,	Folio.	1	Paris,	1852	B.	L 3
Fortier,	Coutume de Paris Conféré, avec les autres Coutumes de France,	Folio.	1	Paris,	1666	A.	M 1
Foster,	On Scire Facias,	8vo.	1	London,	1851	B.	N 7
"	Crown Law,	8vo.	1	"	1809	B.	A 5
Foucart,	Reports and Crown Law,	8vo.	1	Oxford,	1762	A.	
Fonmaur,	Elemens de Droit Public et Administratif,	8vo.	3	Paris,	1843	A.	C 2
Fournel,	Des Droits de Lods et Ventes,	4to.	2 in 1	Lyons,	1783	B.	J 5
"	Du Voisinage,	8vo.	2	Paris,	1834	A.	
Fox,	On Contracts and Assumpsit,	12mo.	1	London,	1842	B.	

Author	Title	Size	No.	Place	Date		Mark
Foy (General),	Discours du,	8vo.	2	Paris,	1826	B.	H 2
France,	Documents relatifs au Régime Hypothecaire,	8vo.	3	Paris,	1844	B.	K 6
"	Tarif des Douanes,	4to.	1	"	1853	B.	U 4
Fregier,	Paraphrase Grecque des Instituts de Justinien,	8vo.	1	Paris,	1847	B.	J 3
Fremery,	Droit Commercial,	8vo.	1	Paris,	1833	B.	M 7
Freminville,	Dictionnaire de la Police Générale,	4to.	1	Paris,	1758	B.	C 4
"	Du Gouvernement des Biens des Communautés d'Habitants,	4to.	5	"	1760	B.	D 5
"	Pratique Universelle des Terriers,	8vo.		"	1762—77	B.	K 4
"	Organisation et Competence des Cours d'Appel,	8vo.	2	Clermont,	1848	B.	B 5
Fremy, Ligneville,	Minorité et Tutelle,	8vo.	2	Paris,	1845	B.	E 3
Fribourg,	Dictionnaire Général des Actes sous Seing Privé,	8vo.	2 in 1	Paris,	1850	A.	R 6
Friesleben,	Constitution de la Ville et Republique de,	8vo.	1	Fribourg,	1816	B.	U 6
Froland,	Corpus Juris Civilis,	4to.	2 in 1	Coloniæ Munatianæ,	1789	A.	A 6
"	Sur le Senatûs Consultûs Velleien,	4to.	1	Paris,	1722	B.	A 6
"	Memoire Concernant la Nature et Qualité des Statuts,	4to.	2	"	1729	A.	A 6
Fry,	Report of Case of Canadian Prisoners,	8vo.	1	London,	1839	B.	K 5
Furgole,	Des Testaments,	4to.	4	Paris,	1745—8	A.	D 5
"	De la Seigneurie Féodale,	18mo.	1	"	1767	B.	C
"	Sur l'Ordonnance de Louis XV. sur les Substitutions,	4to.	1	"	1775	A.	D 5

Author.	Subject.	Size.	No. of Vols.	Where Published.	When.	Library.	Shelf.
Gabriel,	Des Preuves, (bound with Solon,)	8vo.	1	Paris,	1845	B.	K 4
Gale and Davison,	Reports, Q. B., 4 Vic., (1841)—6 Vic., (1843),	8vo.	3	London,	1842—3	A.	P 3
Galiani,	Principes du Droit Public Maritime; see Lucchesi-Palli,						
Galisset et Mignon,	Des Vices Rédhibitoires,	8vo.	1	Paris,	1853	B.	D 2
Ganeau,	Dictionnaire Universel,	Folio.	6	Paris,	1752	A.	s 1
Gauret,	Stile du Conseil du Roy,	4to.	1	Paris,	1700	A.	K 6
Gayot de Pitaval,	Causes Célèbres,	18mo.	22	La Haye,	1735—45	B.	I 2
Genty,	Partages d'Ascendants, (bound with Benech,)	8vo.	1	Paris,	1850	B.	B 1
Gervaise,	Des Contributions Directes,	8vo.	1	Paris,	1847	B.	Q 7
Ghevrel,	Droit Belgique,	4to.	1	Lille,	1736	A.	L 5
Gibelin,	Sur le Droit Civil des Hindous,	8vo.	1	Pondichéry,	1846	A.	K 6
Gilbert,	On Evidence,	8vo.	2 in 1	London,	1791	B.	F 6
Gillet,	Arrêts et Règlements Concernant les Procureurs, &c.,	4to.	4	Paris,	1717	B.	C 4
Gin,	Analyse Raisonnée du Droit Français,	4to.	1	Paris,	1782	B.	S 3
Ginouilhac,	Histoire du Régime Dotale,	8vo.	1	Paris,	1842	A.	U 4
Giraud,	Revue Bibliographique, &c., de Droit Français,	8vo.	in	Aix,	1853	B.	N
"	Sur le Droit de Propriété,	8vo.	1	Paris, Aix,	1838	B.	U 5
"	Histoire du Droit Romain,	8vo.	1	Paris,	1847	A.	J 3
"	Précis de l'Ancien Droit,	8vo.	1	Paris,	1852	A.	L 4
Glyn and Jameson,	Reports, Bankruptcy, 2 Geo. 4, (1821)—9 Geo. 4, (1828).	S. 4to.	2	London,	1824—8	A.	P 4
Gothofredus,	De Regulis Juris,	8vo.	4	Geneva,	1652	B.	L 2
Goujet et Merger,	Dictionnaire de Droit Commercial,	8vo.	1	Paris,	1852	B.	c
Gould,	On Pleading,	8vo.	1	Burlington,	1849	A.	L 5
Graham,	Reports at N. P., C. P., 59 Geo. 3, (1818)—1 Geo. 4, (1820),	8vo.	3	London,	1828	B.	D 3
Green,	On New Trials,	12mo.	1	Albany,	1855	B.	E 4
Grant,	Bankrupt Law,	8vo.	1	London,	1769	B.	E 5
"	Chancery Reports,	8vo.	3	Toronto,	1850	A.	E 7
Greenleaf,	On Evidence,	8vo.	3	Boston,	1848—53	A.	A 2
Grellet, Dumazeau,	De la Defamation,	8vo.	1	Paris,	1847	B.	A 7
Grenier,	Sur l'Edit portant Création de Conservateurs des Hypothèques,	8vo.	2 in 1	Riom,	1787	B.	A 4
"	Des Donations,	18mo.	1	Riom, Paris,	1826	B.	A 6
"	Des Hypothèques,	4to.	2	Clermont-Ferraud,	1829	A.	D 2
Grimaudet,	Œuvres,	S. Fol.	1	Amiens,	1669	B.	A 7
Grimstone,	Reports; see Croke,						
Grosley,	Recherches pour l'Histoire du Droit Français,	18mo.	1	Paris,	1752	B.	st
Grotius,	On War and Peace,	Folio.	1	London,	1738	A.	
"	De Jure Belli ac Pacis,	8vo.	2	Amstelædami,	1720	A.	
"	Droit de la Guerre et de la Paix,	4to.	2	Leyden,	1768	A.	
Grün et Joliat,	Des Assurances Terrestres,	8vo.	1	Paris,	1828	A.	
Gunain,	On Tolls,	8vo.	1	London,	1833	B.	
Guenois,	Conférence des Coutumes,	Folio.	1	Paris,	1618	B.	
"	Conférence des Ordonnances et Edits Royaux,	Folio.	3	"	1660	A.	

Guérard,	Polyptique de l'Abbé Irminon,	4to.	2 in 1	Paris,	1844	B.	B 6
Gueret,	Questions Notables de Droit,	Folio.	1	Paris,	1679	A.	H 7
Guimar,	Des Usages Locaux,	8vo.	1	St. Brienc, Paris,	1846	B.	E 3
Guiné,	De la Répresentation du Double Lien,	4to.	1	Paris,	1727	A.	D 5
"	Répresentation, Double Lien, &c.,	4to.	1	"	1727	B.	D 5
"		12mo.	1	"	1773	B.	D 3
Guyot,	Des Fiefs, &c.,	4to.	7	Paris,	1746—58	A.	D 3
"	Institutes Féodales,	12mo.	1	"	1753	B.	C 5
"	Repertoire de Jurisprudence,	4to.	in 17	"	1784—5	A.	C 0
Guy Pape,	Jurisprudence,	4to.	1	Grenoble, Paris,	1769		f1 F 6

Author	Subject	Size	No. of Vols.	Where Published	When	Library	Shelf
Haggard,	Reports, Admiralty, 1825—1832,	8vo.	in 3	London,	1833	A.	N
Hale,	Pleas of the Crown,	8vo.	2	London,	{1, 1800; 2, 1788}	B.	M 5
"	History of Common Law,	8vo.	1	"	1820	A.	L 3
"	Natura Brevium,	8vo.	1	Dublin,	1793	A.	b 1
Hammond,	Digested Index to Term Reports, &c., during Geo. 3,	8vo.	2	London,	1819	A.	B 4
Hauih,	Des Conséquences des Condemnations Pénales,	8vo.	1	Paris,	1848	B.	B 4
Hansard,	On Aliens,	8vo.	1	London,	1844	B.	P 6
Hardwicke, Lord C. J.,	Cases, 7 Geo. 2, (1733)—10 Geo. 2, (1736)	Folio.	1	"	1770	A.	h 1
Harper,	Universal Gazetteer,	4to.	1	New York,	1855	A.	R 1
Harris and McHenry,	Maryland Reports, 1700, Revolution,	8vo.	1	"	1809	A.	L 3
Harrison,	Chancery,	8vo.	2	Dublin,	1791	A.	b 1
"	Digest of Cases in H. of Lords & Courts of Com. Law, 1756—1829	8vo.	2	London,	1829	A.	b 1
"	Do. do., and Bankruptcy and Crown Cases, 1756—1836	8vo.	3	"	1837	A.	R 4
"	Condensed Reports, Superior Court of Orleans and Supreme Court of Louisiana, 1809—1830,	8vo.	4	New Orleans,	1839—40	A.	R 6
Haskell and Smith,	Gazetteer of United States,	8vo.	1	New York,	1843	A.	P 6
Hatsell,	Precedents in House of Commons,	4to.	4	London,	1785	A.	A 5
Hautefeuille,	Droits et Devoirs des Nations Neutres,	8vo.	4	Paris,	1848—9	B.	M 7
Hawkins,	Pleas of the Crown,	Folio.	1	London,	1762	A.	M 5
"	"	8vo.	1	"	1777	A.	M 5
"	"	8vo.	2	"	1824	A.	U 4
Heinneceius,	Recitationes,	8vo.	2	Parisiis,	1810	A.	U 2
"	Elements du Droit Civil Romain,	12mo.	4	Paris,	1812	A.	A
Henke,	Droit Public de la Suisse,	8vo.	1	Genève, Paris,	1825	A.	B 4
Henrion,	Code Ecclésiastique Français,	8vo.	2 in 1	Paris,	1829	B.	C 5
Henrion de Pansey,	Dissertations Féodales,	4to.	1	"	1789	A.	C
"	Traité des Fiefs,	4to.	2	"	1773	B.	C 1
Henriquez,	Code des Seigneurs,	18mo.	1	"	1786	A.	G 7
Henri,	Code,	8vo.	4	Paris,	1738	A.	A 1
Henris,	Œuvres,	Folio.	8	London,	1820—51	B.	C
Hertsle,	Collection of Treaties and Conventions,	8vo.	8	London,	1788	A.	C 6
Hervé,	Théorie de Matières Féodales et Censuelles,	18mo.	3	Paris,	1745—8	A.	R 1
Hevin,	Coutume de Bretagne,	4to.	6	Rennes,	1842—5	B.	D 2
Hill,	Reports, Superior Court of New York, 1841—1844,	8vo.	1	Albany, New York,	1846	R.	B 3
Hindmarsh,	On Patents,	8vo.	1	London,	1848	R.	D 2
Hirer,	Histoire des Institutions Judiciares de la France, 1780—1848,	8vo.	1	Paris,	1847	B.	b 1
Hodges,	On Railways and Railway Companies,	8vo.	1	London,	1848	A.	O 6
Holcombe,	Digest of Supreme Court of United States,	L. 8vo.	1	New York,	1738	B.	P 4
Holt, Lord C. J.,	Reports, K. B., 1 W. & M. (1688)—(1710),	Folio.	1	In the Savoy,	1738	A.	
Holt,	Report at N. P., C. P., 55 Geo. 3, (1815)—58 Geo. 3, (1817)	8vo.	1	London,	1818	A.	

Author	Title	Size	No.	Place	Date		Shelf
Holtius,	Analyse Historique du Droit d'Accroisement,	8vo.	1	Liège,	1830	B.	C 4
Houàrd,	Sur les Coutumes Anglo-Normandes,	4to.	4	Rouen,	1776	B.	O 6
"	Anciennes Loix des Français,	4to.	2	"	1766	B.	D 7
"	Dictionnaire de la Coutume de Normandie,	4to.	4	"	1780—2	B.	C 6
Howard,	Reports, Supreme Court of United States, 1843—1851,	8vo.	13	{1—3, Philadelphia}{4-13, Boston}	1843—52	A.	{Q 1 and Q 2}
Howell,	State Trials, 9 Hen. 2, (1163)—19 Geo. 3, (1179),	..8vo.	21	London,	1816	A.	M 6
Hughes,	On Extent: Report of King vs. Beth et al.,	8vo.	2	London,	1811	A.	L 3
Hullock,	Law of Costs,	8vo.	2	"	1810	A.	L 3
Hulot et Berthelot,	Digeste de Justinien,	4to.	7	"	1805	A.	U 6
Hume,	Laws of the Customs,	8vo.	1	Metz, Paris,	1805	A.	J 2
Hunt,	Merchant's Magazine,	8vo.	36	London,	1836	A.	J K 1
Husson,	Législation des Travaux Publics,	8vo.	1	New York,	1839—57	B.	A
Huzard et Harel,	De la Garantie et des Vices Rédhibetoires,	12mo.	1	Paris,	1851	B.	D 3

Author.	Subject.	Size.	No. of Vols.	Where Published.	When.	Library.	Shelf.
Isambert, ...	Récueil Général des Anciennes Loix Françaises, 420—1789,......	8vo.	29	Paris, ...	1822—7	A.	D

Author	Title	Size	No.	Place	Year		Shelf
Jacob,	Conveyancer,	12mo.	1	In the Savoy,	1715	A.	L 3
"	New Law Dictionary,	Folio.	1	London,	1772	A.	P 7
Jacquel,	Coutume de Touraine,	4to.	2	Auxerre, Paris,	1761	A.	D 6
Jay,	Des Scellés,	8vo.	1	Paris,	1847	B.	K 4
Jeremy,	Law of Carriers,	8vo.	1	London,	1815	A.	J 2
Johnson,	Reports, Supreme Court of New York, 1806—1823,	8vo.	in 20	{ 1–11, Philadelp'a, } { 12—20, Albany, }	1832 } 1816—23 }	A.	Q 23
Jouanneau et Solon,	Discussion du Code Napoléon,	4to.	3	Paris,	1808	A.	G 4
Jousse,	Des Fonctions des Commissaires,	18mo.	1	"	1759	A.	K 2
"	Nouveau Commentaire sur l'Edit d'Avril, 1695,	18mo.	1	"	1757	A.	B 2
"	De la Jurisdiction des Officiaux,	18mo.	1	"	1769	A.	B 3
"	Des Fonctions des Commissaires Enqueteurs Examinateurs,	18mo.	1	"	1759	A.	
"	De la Jurisdiction des Presidiaux,	18mo.	1	"	1764	A.	K 2
"	Gouvernement des Paroisses,	18mo.	in	"	1769	A.	B 3
"	Administration de la Justice,	4to.	1	"	1771	A.	
"	Sur l'Ordonnance du Commerce, 1673,	8vo.	2	Poitiers,	1828	B.	J 3
Jousselin,	Nouveau Commentaire sur l'Ordonnance Civile, 1667,	12mo.	2	Paris,	1767	A.	K 3
"	Des Servitudes d'Utilité Publique,	8vo.	2	Paris,	1850	B.	C 2
Justininuus,	Institutiones,	12mo.	1	Lugduni Batavorum,	1733	A.	U 5

F.

Author.	Subject	Size.	No. of Vols.	Where Published.	When.	Library.	Shelf.
Kant,	Principes Metaphysiques du Droit,	8vo.	1	Paris,	1853	B.	A 1
Kelham,	Norman Dictionary,	8vo.	1	London,	1779	B.	g
Kelly,	On Life Annuities,	8vo.	1	"	1835	B.	J 5
Kent,	Commentaries on American Law,	8vo.	4	New York,	1832	A.	a 1
Klimrath,	Histoire du Droit Français,	8vo.	2 in 1	Paris, Strasbourg,	1843	B.	B 3
Klüber,	Droit des Gens,	8vo.	2 in 1	Paris, Rio de Janeiro,	1831	B.	A 5
Knapp,	Reports, Privy Council, 1829—1836,	8vo	3	London,	1831—7	A.	P 5

Author.	Subject.	Size.	No. of Vols.	Where Published.	When.	Library.	Shelf.
Lachize,	Expropriation Forcée,	8vo.	2	Paris,	1829	B.	C 2
Lacretelle,	Discours sur le Préjugé des Peines Infamantes, &c.,	8vo.	1		1784	B.	M 1
Laferrière,	Histoire du Droit Français,	8vo.	4		1852—3	B.	B 3
Laget de Podio,	Sur les Assurances Maritimes,	8vo.	2 in 1		1847	B.	J 5
Luthaye et al.,	Code Civil Annoté,	4to.	1	Marseille,	1843	B.	G 5
Lalaure,	Des Servitudes Réelles,	4to.	1	Paris,	1786	A.	C 2
"	"	8vo.	1	Caen,	1827	A.	C 2
"	"	8vo.	1	Paris,	1827	P.	C 2
Lalleau,	De l'Expropriation,	8vo.	2	"	1845	A.	C 2
Lange,	La Nouvelle Pratique,	4to.	1	"	1755	A.	K 6
Langlois,	Des Droits des Conseillers du Roy, Notaires, &c.,	4to.	1	"	1738	A.	L 6
Lapeyrière,	Décisions Sommaires du Palais,	4to.	2	Bordeaux, Paris,	1808	A.	H 6
Laplacee,	Dictionnaire des Fiefs,	8vo.	1	Paris,	1757	A.	C
Laselles,	Liber Hibernie, 1152—1824,	Folio.	2	London,	1824	A.	r 1
Latruffe, Montmeylian,	Des Droits des Communes,	8vo.	1	Paris,	1825	B.	B 2
Lavenas,	Des Vices Rédhibitoires,	12mo.	1	"	1838	B.	D 2
Lawes,	On Charter Parties,	8vo.	1	London,	1813	A.	J 2
"	Crown Law,	8vo.	2	"	1800	A.	J 2
Leach,	Code des Etrangers,	8vo.	1	Londres,	1849	A.	M 1
LeBaron,	Des Successions,	8vo.	1	Paris,	1714	B.	B 4
LeBrun,	"	Folio.	1	"	1775	A.	D 7
"	De l'Etat des Personnes,	Folio.	1		1774	A.	D 7
LeCoq,	Dictionary of Practice,	18mo.	2 in 1	Rouen,	1825	A.	B 4
Lee,	On Shipping and Insurance,	8vo.	2	London,	1854	B.	L 4
Lees,	De Origine et Progressu Juris Civilis Romani,	12mo.	1	Liverpool,	1672	A.	J 2
Leewius,	Memoires sur les Matières Domaniales,	8vo.	1	Lugdeni Batavorum,	1764	A.	U 5
Lefevre de la Planche,	Code des Etrangers,	4to.	3	Paris,	1832	B.	B 6
Legat,	De la Legislation des Portions Communales,	8vo.	1	"	1854	B.	B 4
Letientil,	Coutume de Troyes,	8vo.	1	Paris,	1715	B.	A 4
LeGrand,	Les Coutumes de Flandre,	Folio.	3	Cambray,	1699	B.	C 7
"	Plaidoyez et Harangues,	Folio.	1	Paris,	1741	B.	B 7
LeMaistre,	Coutume de Paris,	4to.	3	"	1851—5	B.	H 3
"	Décisions des Tribunaux Bas Canada,	Folio.	1	Quebec,	1856	A.	D 7
"	Reports of Seigniorial Court,	Folio.	5		1819	B.	c
Lelievre et Angers,	Fins de Nen-Recevoir,	8vo.	2		1821	B.	c
"	Lois des Batiments, ou Nouveau Desgodets,	8vo.	1	Nantes,	1852	A.	K 3
Lemerie,	Introduction à l'Histoire du Droit,	8vo.	2	Paris,	1835	B.	B 2
Lepage,	Dictionnaire du Digeste,	8vo.	1	"	1808—9	B.	D 2
Lerminier,	Revue de Législation et de Jurisprudence,	8vo.	2	"	1846—8	A.	D 2
Lesparat et Dussan,		4to.	2	"		A.	A 2
Letourneaux, Lelievre et Angers,		8vo.	3	Montreal and Quebec.		A.	U 6

Author	Title	Size	Vols.	Place	Date		Shelf
Levinz,	Reports, C. B., 12 Car. 2, (1661)—8 Wm. 3, (1696)	S. Fol.	1	London,	1702	A.	O 7
Lowndes,	Index to Statutes at large, Mag. Char., 1830,	8vo.	1	"	1831	A.	c 1
Lilly,	Modern Entries, K. B., C. P., and Ex.,	Folio.	1	In the Savoy,	1741	A.	L 7
"	Entries,	8vo.	in 2	Dublin,	1792	A.	L
Lingue,	Theorie des Loix Civiles,	18mo.	2	Londres,	1767	A.	N 6
Littleton,	Reports, C. B. and Ex., 2 Car. 1, (1626)—7 Car. 1, (1632)	Folio.	1	London,	1683	A.	U 1
Livius,	Historiæ,	12mo.	7	Londini,	1749	A.	H 3
L'Hospital,	Œuvres Complètes,	8vo.	3	Paris,	1824–5	B.	H 3
"	Œuvres Inédites,	8vo.	2	"	1825	B.	F 3
Locré,	Esprit du Code Civil,	8vo.	7	"	1807—14	A.	J 4
"	Esprit du Code de Commerce,	8vo.	4	"	1829	B.	F & G 3
"	Legislation Civile, Commerciale et Criminelle de la France,	8vo.	31	"	1827—32	B.	A 3
Lorieux,	De la Prerogative Royale,	8vo.	2	"	1840	B.	R 4
Louisiana,	Civil Code,	8vo.	1	New Orleans,	1838	A.	K 7
"	Report to Code of Evidence,	Folio.	1	"	1678	A.	
Loyseau,	Œuvres,	Folio.	1	Paris,	1652	B.	G 7
Loisel,	Opuscules,	4to.	2 in 1	"	1846	B.	E 6
Loysel,	Institutes Coutumières,	12mo.	2	"	1793	B.	A 3
Lucas,	Du Système Pénal,	12mo.	1	"	1827	B.	M 2
"	Du Système Penitentiaire en Europe et Etats Unis,	8vo.	2	"	1834	A.	M 2
"	De la Réforme des Prisons,	8vo.	3	"	1836	B.	N 2
Lucchesi-Palli,	Du Droit Public Maritime,	8vo.	1	"	1842		A 4
Lucet,	Principes du Droit Canonique Universel,	4to.	1	"	1788		B 5
Lush,	Practice of Courts at Westminster,	8vo.	1	London,	1840		L 4
Letwyche,	On Pleading the General Issue,	12mo.	1	"	1842		L 4

Author.	Subject.	Size.	No. of Vols.	Where Published.	When.	Library.	Shelf.
Mackay,	Montreal Directory, 1848-52-53,	12mo.	3	Montreal,	1848—53	B.	e 1
Mackeldy,	Manuel de Droit Romain,	8vo.	1	Bruxelles,	1841	B.	U 4
Mackintosh,	On Law of Nature and Nations,	12mo.	1	London,	1828	A.	A 5
Macnally,	Rules of Evidence,	8vo.	2	"	1802	B.	M 3
Macnamara,	On Nullities and Irregularities in law,	12mo.	1	"	1842	B.	K 3
Macqueen,	Practice of House of Lords and Privy Council,	L. 8vo.	1	"	1842	B.	
Maulock,	On Husband and Wife,	8vo.	6 in 3	Philadelphia,	1849	B.	C 4
Mailhot de Chassat,	Reports, Chancery, 1815—1822,	8vo.	2 in 1	Paris,	1829	A.	N 2
"	Le Retroactivité des Lois,	8vo.	1	"	1845	B.	A
Maleclay-la-Mothe,	Des Statuts,	8vo.	1	"	1845	B.	A
Malepeyre et Jourdain,	Questions de Droit,	18mo.	1	"	1770	B.	A
Maleville,	Des Sociétés Commerciales,	8vo.	1	"	1833	B.	J 3
	Discussion du Code Civil; see DeMaleville.						
Mangin,	De l'Action Publique,						
Manning, jr.,	On Law of Nations,	8vo.	2	Paris,	1844	B.	K 4
Manning and Ryland,	Reports, K. B. 8 Geo. 4, (1827)—11 Geo. 4, (1830),	8vo.	1	London,	1839	B.	A 5
Manning and Granger,	Reports, C. P, 3 Vic, (1840)—8 Vic, (1845),	8vo.	5	"	1828—37	A.	P
Manning, Granger and Scott,	Common Bench Reports, 8 Vic, (1845)—12 Vic, (1849),	8vo.	7	"	1841—6	A.	N 5 & O 1
Marbeau,	Des Transactions, &c.,	8vo.	1	"	1846—50	A.	O 1
Marnier,	Etablissements et Coutumes, &c., de l'Echiquier de Normandie, 1207—1245,	8vo.	1	Paris,	1832	B.	D 2
	Le Conseil de Pierre DeFontaines; vide Pierre DeFontaines.						
Marsonier,	Histoire de la Contrainte par Corps,	8vo.	1	Paris,	1839	B.	E 2
Martens,	Causes Celebres du Droit des Gens,	8vo.	2 in 1	Paris,	1843	B.	K 4
"	Nouvelles Causes Celebres du Droit des Gens,	8vo.	2 in 1	Leipzig, Paris,	1827	B.	A 5
"	Le Guide Diplomatique,	8vo.	2 in 1	"	1843	B.	A 5
Martin,	Reports, S. C., Louisiana,	8vo.	10	New Orleans,	1854	A.	A 3
Martin,	Lord Tenterden's Act, (9 Geo. II, c. 14,),	12mo.	1	London,	1846—52	B.	R 2
Martin du Nord,	Documens Relatifs au Régime Hypothécaire,	8vo.	3	Paris,	1829	B.	L 3
Massabiau,	Manuel du Procureur du Roy,	8vo.	3	"	1814	B.	E 5
Massé,	Le Parfait Notaire,	4to.	3	"	1843	B.	K 4
"	Dictionnaire du Contentieux Commercial,	8. J.	1	"		B.	L 6
Massol,	Droit Commercial,	8vo.	6	"	1840	B.	J 6
Masson,	De la Separation de Corps,	8vo.	1	"	1844—5	B.	J 3
Maubuy (Aublet de),	Des Locations en Garn,	8vo.	1	"	1841	B.	C 2
Manle and Selwyn,	Traités des Dépôts; see Aublet DeMaubuy,	8vo.	1	"	1847	B.	C 1
May,	On Parliament,	8vo.	in 5	London,	1814—23	A.	O 5
Meaume,	Des Droits d'Usage dans les Forêts,	8vo.	1	London,	1851	B.	
Meeson and Welsby,	Reports, Ex., 6 Wm. 4, (1836)—10 Vic. (1847),	8vo.	2	Paris,	1851	A.	C 3
Menochius,	De Arbitrariis Judicum, &c.,	8vo.	16	Philadelphia,	1847—52	A.	O 2
"	De Adipiscenda, Retinenda, et Recuperanda Possessione,	Folio.	2 in 1	Lugduni,	1606	A.	R 7
"		Folio.	1	Genevæ,	1629	A.	R 7

Author	Title	Size	No.	Place	Date		
Menochius,	De Præsumptionibus,	Folio.	2	Moulins,	1670	A.	R7
Méplain,	Du Bail a Portion de Fruits,	8vo.	1	London,	1850	E.	C1
Merivale,	Reports, Chancery, 55 Geo. 3, [1815]—57 Geo. 3, [1816],	8vo.	in 18	Paris,	1817—19	A.	N2
Merlin,	Repertoire de Jurisprudence,	4to.	18	Paris,	1807—25	A.	G1
"	Recueil des Questions de Droit,	4to.	9	"	1810—30	A.	G1
Merlin et Bondonneau,	Table Générale au Repertoire de Jurisprudence,	4to.	1	"	1829	A.	G1
Meslé,	Traité des Minorité, Tutelles, &c.,	4to.	1	"	1755	B.	B5
Mey,	Maximes du Droit Public François,	4to.	1	"	1775	A.	A6
Meyer,	Esprit, Origine et Progrès des Institutions Judiciares,	8vo.	2 in 1	Amsterdam,	1823	A.	A2
Mignet,	De la Feodalité,	S. 8vo.	in 5	Paris,	1822	A.	B3
Miller and Curry, 1-5 6-19	Louisiana Reports, 1830—1841,	8vo.	19	New Orleans,	1831—42	A.	R3
Minier,	Précis Historique,	8vo.	1	Paris,	1834—5	B.	H2
Mirabeau,	Œuvres,	8vo.	8	Parisiis,	1539	A.	D6
Molenlincrs,	Commentarius in Consuetudines Parisienses,	Folio.	1	"	1681	A.	E7
Molinæus,	Opera,	Folio.	5	Paris,	1853	B.	J2
Mollot,	Bourses de Commerce,	8vo.	1	London,	1701	A.	A4
Molloy,	De Jure Maritimo,	8vo.	1	Montreal,	1841	A.	h
Monlert,	On Education,	8vo.	1	London,	1822	A.	J3
Montagu,	On Partnership,	8vo.	2	London,	1832	A.	N
"	Reports, Bankruptcy, 1 Geo. 4, (1829)—2 Wm. 4, (1833),	8vo.	1	"	1834—9	A.	N
Montagu and Ayrton,	Reports, Bankruptcy, 3 Wm. 4, (1833)—1 Vic., (1838),	8vo.	3	"	"	A.	N
Montagu and Bligh,	Reports, Bankruptcy, 3 Wm. 4, (1832),	8vo.	1	"	1835	A.	N
Montagu, Deacon and DeGex,	Reports, Bankruptcy, 3 Vic., (1840)—7 Vic, (1844),	8vo.	3	"	1842—5	A.	N
Montagu and Chitty,	Reports, Bankruptcy, 1 Vic., (1838)—3 Vic, (1840),	8vo.	1	"	1840	B.	N
Montagu and MacArthur,	Reports, Chancery, 9 Geo. 4, (1826)—11 Geo. 4, (1828),	4to.	1	"	1830	B.	H3
Montesquieu,	Œuvres Complètes,	18mo.	1	Paris,	1853	A.	M1
Montluc,	Instruction Facile sur les Conventions,	12mo.	1	Montreal,	1811	B.	M4
Montreal, King's Bench,	Rules of Practice, 1811,	8vo.	3	Paris,	1829	A.	P4
Montreau,	De la Jurisprudence Anglaises sur les Crimes Politiques,	8vo.	1	London,	1837—44	A.	P4
Moody,	Crown Cases, 1824—1844,	8vo.	2	"	1831	A.	d1
Moody and Malkin,	Reports at N. P., K. B., C. P., 7 Geo. 4, (1826)—1 Wm. 4, (1830),	8vo.	1	"	1837—44	A.	N4
Moody and Robinson,	Reports at N. P., K. B., C. P. & Ex., 1 Wm. 4 (1830)—7 Vic. (1844),	8vo.	2	"	1816	A.	P5
Moore,	Index to Term Reports, 1785—1814,	8vo.	5	"	1828—32	A.	M2
Moore and Payne,	Reports, C. P. and Ex., 8 Geo. 4, (1827)—1 Wm. 4, (1831),	8vo.	4	"	1833—1	A.	M2
Moore and Scott,	Reports, C. P. Ex. & H. of Lords, 2 W. 4, (1831)—1 W. 4 (1833),	8vo.	6	"	"	A.	A3
Moore,	Reports, Privy Council, 1836—1849,	8vo.	1	Paris,	1837	A.	A1
Moreau, Christophe,	De l'Etat Actuel en Personnes en France,	8vo.	1	"	1838	P.	L3
"	De la Réforme des Prisons,	8vo.	1	"	1853	B.	K4
Moreul,	Manuel des Agens Consulaires,	8vo.	1	"	1853	B.	M5
"	Recueil de Traités Diplomatiques,	8vo.	2 in 1	Dublin,	1787	B.	Q7
Morgan,	Attorney's Vade Mecum,	8vo.	1	Paris,	1847	B.	R7
Morin,	De la Discipline des Cours et Tribunaux,	4to.	1	"	1850—1	A.	R7
"	Répertoire du Droit Criminel,	Folio.	2	Paris, Blaye,	1848	B.	E4
Morineau,	Essai sur les Etats Unis d'Amerique,	Folio.	2	Paris, Blaye,	1848	B.	E4
Mornacius,	Observationes in 24 Priores Libros Digestorum,	Folio.	2	Latebæ Parisiorum,	1654	A.	R7
"	Observationes in 4 Libros Codicis,	Folio.	2	"	1654	A.	R7
Mourlon,	Des Subrogations Personnelles,	8vo.	1	Paris,	1848	B.	E4

Author.	Subject.	Size.	No. of Vols.	Where Published.	When.	Library.	Shelf.
Nadault de Buffon,	Usines sur les Cours d'Eau,	8vo.		Paris,	1852	B.	C 1
Nelson,	Rights of the Clergy,	12mo.	1	London,	1715	A.	B 4
Nevile and Manning,	Reports, K. B., 5 Wm. 4, (1835)—6 Wm. 4, (1836).	8vo.		"	1836	A.	
Neuville (DeBréard),	Pandectes de Justinien; see Pothier.						
Nevile and Perry,	Reports, K. B. and Exc., 7 Wm. 4, (1836)—1 Vic., (1838).	8vo.	3	London,	1837—8	A.	P 2 3
Nevile and Manning,	Reports, K. B. and Exc., 3 Wm. 4, (1832)—6 Wm. 4, (1835).	8vo.	in 6	"	1834—9	A.	P 1
Nicolini,	Droit Pénal,	8vo.	1	Paris,	1851	B.	M 2
Noblet,	Du Compte Courant,	8vo.	1	"	1848	B.	J 5
Nood†,	Opera Omnia,	4to.	1	Lugduni Batavorum,	1713	A.	U 5
Nongarede,	Histoire des Loix sur le Mariage et Divorce,	8vo.	2	Paris,	1803	A.	C 3
Nouguier,	Des Lettres de Change,	8vo.	2	Paris,	1851	B.	J 4
Nova Scotia,	Statutes at Large, 32 Geo. 2, (1758)—44 Geo. 3, (1804)	4to.	1	Halifax,	1805	A.	c 1

Author.	Subject.	Size.	No. of Vols.	Where Published.	When.	Library.	Shelf.
Oke,	Magisterial Formulist,	8vo.	1	London,	1850	B.	L 4
"	Magisterial Synopsis,	8vo.	1	"	1853	B.	M 3
Oldfield,	On Parliaments,	8vo.	1	"	1797	A.	A 2
"	Representative History of Great Britain and Ireland,	8vo.	6	"	1816	A.	A
Omer et Talon,	Œuvres,	8vo.	6	Paris,	1821	B.	H 3
Orillard,	De la Compétence des Tribunaux de Commerce,	8vo.	1	"	1844	B.	K 5
Ortolan,	Régles Internationales et Diplomatie de la Mer,	8vo.	2 in 1	"	1853	B.	A 4
Otto,	Thesaurus Juris Romani,	Folio.	5	Trajecti ad Rhenum,	1733	A.	S 7
Ovid,	Metamorphosis,	8vo.	1			A.	U 5

Author	Subject	Size	No. of Vols.	Where Published	When	Library	Shelf
Pages,	De la Responsabilité des Notaires,	8vo.	1	Montpellier, Paris,	1843	B.	K 3
Paillet,	Des Successions,	8vo.	3	Paris,	1821	B.	D 4
Paley,	On Principal and Agent,	8vo.	1	London,	1819	A.	J 2
Palin,	Coutume de Touraine,	4to.	2	Tours,	1661	A.	D 6
Papon,	Arrests Notables des Cours Souveraines,	4to.	1			A.	H 6
Pardessus,	Collection de Lois Maritimes,	4to.	3	Paris,	1828—34	B.	J 6
"	Des Servitudes,	8vo.	2	"	1841—?	B.	C 2
"	Droit Commercial,	8vo.	6	"		B.	J 4
Parent, DuChatelet,	Loi Salique,	4to.	1	"	1843	B.	B 6
Park,	De la Prostitution,	8vo.	2	"	1837	B.	C 2
"	On Marine Insurance,	8vo.	1	London,	1787	A.	J 5
Parker,	Criminal Reports,	8vo.	2	London,	1817	A.	M 3
Parry,	On Lord Campbell's Libel Act,	8vo.	1	Albany,	1855	A.	M 3
Pasquier,	Œuvres,	12mo.	2	London,	1844	B.	G 7
Pastoret,	Interpretation des Institutes de Justinien,	Folio.	2	Amsterdam,	1723	R.	U 6
"	Zoroastre, Confucius et Mahomet comparé,	4to.	1	Paris,	1847	R.	T 2
"	Des Loix Pénales,	8vo.	2 in 1	"	1788	B.	M 2
Patru,	Œuvres diverses,	8vo.	2	"	1790	B.	G 6
Paul,	Des Droits du Mari,	4to.	1	"	1714	B.	C 4
Paule de la Garde,	Des Droits du Souverain en France,	8vo.	1	"	1847	B.	B 6
Pearce,	History of the Inns of Court,	4to.	1	London,	1767	B.	H 1
"	On Convocation,	8vo.	2	"	1848	B.	B 4
Pellat,	Law of Indictments,	12mo.	1	"	1848	B.	M 4
Peleus,	Institutes de Gains, (bound with Domeuget)	8vo.	1	Paris,	1851	B.	H 6
Penruddocke,	Questions Illustres,	4to.	1		1844	B.	M 2
Pepin (LeHalleur),	On Criminal Law,	12mo.	1	London,	1605	A.	C 1
Perrault,	Histoire de l'Emphytéose,	8vo.	1	Paris,	1842	A.	A 2
Perreciot,	Lex Parliamentaria,	8vo.	1	London,	1843	B.	B 4
Perrier,	De l'Etat Civil,	8vo.	1	Quebec,	1803	A.	
"	Mémoire,	4to.	3 in 2	Paris,	1845	B.	
Perrin,	Arrêts Notables du Parlement de Dijon,	Folio.	1	Dijon,	1735	A.	H 7
"	Des Nullités du Droit,	8vo.	1	Lons-le-Saulnier,	1816	B.	K 3
Perrot,	Code des Constructions,	8vo.	1	Paris, Bordeaux,	1842	B.	D 2
"	Dictionnaire de Voïerie,	4to.	1	Paris,	1782	B.	D 5
Persil,	Régime Hypothécaire,	8vo.	4	London,	1839—4?	A.	P 3
Perry and Davison,	Reports, Q. B. & Ex., 2 Vic., (1829)—4 Vic., (1841)	8vo.	2	Paris,	1820	A.	E 5
Persil,	Questions sur les Privilèges,	8vo.	1	"	1820	A.	E 5
"	Des Sociétés Commerciales,	8vo.	1	"	1833	B.	J 3
"	De la Lettre de Change,	8vo.	1	"	1837	B.	J 4
Persil et Croissant,	Sur les Commissionnaires et sur les Achats et Ventes,	8vo.	1	"	1836	B.	J 2
Petersdorff,	Abridgment, 1660—4 Geo. 4,	8vo.	15	New York,	1829—32	A.	b

Author	Title	Size	Vols.	Place	Date		Mark
Petersdorff,	General Index to Abridgment,	8vo.	1	London,	1822	A.	a 1
"	Abridgment, 1824—1840,	8vo.	15	"	1825—30	B.	a 1
"	Abridgment, 1824—1840,	8vo.	5	"	1841—4	B.	b
Petit,	Droit Public ou Gouvernement des Colonies Françaises,	8vo.	2	Paris,	1771	A.	K 4
"	Des Surenchères,	8vo.	1	"	1848	A.	Q
Peters,	Reports, Circuit Court of United States, 1803—1842,	8vo.	1	Philadelphia,	1819	A.	Q & Q 1
"	Reports, Supreme Court of United States, 1828—1842,	8vo.	16	{ 1-15, Philadelphia; 16, Boston }	1828—41	A.	C 1
Peyret, Lallier,	Legislation des Mines, &c.,	8vo.	2	Paris,	1842	B.	C 2
Pezzani,	Des Empêchements du Mariage,	8vo.	1	"	1844	B.	C 2
Phillimore,	Reports, Ecclesiastical Courts, 1818—1821,	8vo.	in 3	London,	1838	A.	O 1
Phillips,	Reports, English Eccles. Courts, 49 Geo. 3 (1809)—2 Geo. 4 (1821),	8vo.	3 in 1	Philadelphia,	1827	B.	O 4
"	On Domicile,	8vo.	1	London,	1831	B.	B 4
"	On Evidence,	8vo.	5	Paris,	1847	B.	L 3
"	On Evidence,	8vo.	5	New York,	1849—50	A.	L 5
Piales,	Des Réparations des Eglises,	8vo.	4	Paris,	1843	A.	O 6
Pickering,	Modern Reports, K. B., 2 & 3 Anne, (1704—5),	18mo.	in 6	In the Savoy,	1762	A.	U 4
Picot,	Du Mariage Romain, Chretien et Français,	Folio.	1	Paris,	1757	B.	E 2
Pierre de Fontaine,	Le Conseil de,	8vo.	1	"	1849	B.	K 6
Pigeau,	Procédure Civile,	8vo.	2	"	1846	A.	K 6
"	"	4to.	2	"	1787	B.	K 6
"	"	4to.	2	"	{ 1 v. 1809; 2 v. 1808 }	A.	K 6
"	Des Régales,	4to.	1	"	1837	B.	B 5
Pinson,	Chronology,	4to.	1	Edinburgh,	1688	A.	f.
Playfair,	Reports, Edward 6, Mary, Phillip and Mary, and Elizabeth,	Folio.	2	In the Savoy,	1784	A.	O 7
Plowden,	Règles du Droit Français,	Folio.	1	Paris,	1761	A.	E 3
Poequet de Lironiere,	Contume d'Anjou,	18mo.	1	"	1768	B.	B 7
"	Des Fiefs,	4to.	2	Paris,	1725	B.	C 5
Pollexfen, Sir H.,	Reports and Arguments, K. B., C. P. & Exc., 22 Car. 2 (1671)—36 Car. 2, (1685),	Folio.	1	Paris,	1771	B.	B 7
Poncet,	Des Actions, (Traités élémentaires de Légis., &c.),	8vo.	1	London,	1702	A.	N 6
"	"	8vo.	1	Dijon,	1817	B.	K 3
"	Des Jugements,	8vo.	2	"	1817	B.	K 3
"	"	8vo.	2	"	1821	B.	K 4
Ponsot,	Du Cautionnement,	8vo.	3	"	1822	B.	K 4
Pontas,	Dictionnaire de Cas de Conscience,	8vo.	3	Paris, Dijon,	1844	A.	D 2
Pothier,	Œuvres,	Folio.	8	Paris,	1715	B.	T 7
"	"	4to.	8	Paris, Orleans,	1773—1841	A.	E 4
Poulain DuParc,	Pandectes de Justinien,	4to.	10	Paris, Orleans,	1780—1	B.	E
"	Pandectæ Justinianæ,	8vo.	2	Paris,	1845—8	A.	E 3
"	Coutume d'Orleans,	4to.	3	Orleans,	1773	A.	U 3
"	De la Possession et Prescription,	Folio.	1	Parisiis,	1818—23	A.	R 7
"	Coutumes Générales de Bretagne ; sec Hevin,	18mo.	1	Paris, Orleans,	1818	A.	D 6
"	Journal des Audiences du Parlement de Bretagne,	4to.	5	Rennes,	1787—8	A.	H 6

Author	Subject	Size	No. of Vols.	Where Published	When	Library	Shelf
Poulain DuParc,	Principes du Droit Français (Bretagne),	12mo.	12	Rennes,	1767—71	B.	E 2
Powell,	On Devises,	8vo.	1	London,	1788	A.	D 3
Pratt,	Digested Index to Term Reports—K. B., 1785—1825; C. P., 1788—1825; Exc, 1792—1825,	8vo.	1	London,	1826	A.	b 1
Prideaux,	On Tithes,	8vo.	1	"	1736	A.	B 4
Priestly,	On Government,	8vo.	1	"	1771	A.	A 2
Pritchard,	Digest of Cases in Court of Admiralty,	8vo.	1	"	1847	B.	b 1
Prost de Royer,	Dictionnaire de Jurisprudence et d'Arrets,	4to.	7	Lyon,	1781—8	A.	e
Proudhon,	Du Domaine Public,	8vo.	5	Dijon,	1833—4	A.	B 2
"	Droits d'Usufruit, d'Usage, d'Habitation, et de Superficie,	8vo.	9	"	1824—7	A.	C 3
"	Du Domaine Public,	8vo.	5	"	1833—4	B.	B 2
"	Du Domaine de Propriété,	8vo.	3	"	1839	B.	C 4
"	De l'Etat des Personnes,	8vo.	2	"	1842—3	B.	B 4
Pufendorf,	Droit de la Nature et des Gens,	8vo.	2	Paris,	1848	B.	B 4
"	"	4to.	2	Leide,	1759	A.	A 6
Pulbusque,	Dictionnaire Municipale,	4to.	2	Lyons,	1771	A.	A 6
"		8vo.	1	Paris,	1847	B.	B 2
Pullin,	Law of Attorneys and Solicitors,	12mo.	1	London,	1854	B.	L 3

Author.	Subject.	Size.	No. of Vols.	Where Published.	When.	Library.	Shelf.
Quenault,	Des Assurances Terrestres,	8vo.	1	Paris,	1828	B.	h
Quérard,	La France Littéraire,	8vo.	10	Paris,	1827—39	B.	

Author	Subject	Size.	No. of Vols.	Where Published.	When.	Library.	Shelf.
Rageau,	Les Coutumes de Berri,	Folio.	1	Paris,	1615	B.	B 7
Rapetti,	Li Livres de Justice et de Plet,	4to.	1	"	1850	B.	B 6
Rastell,	Entries,	Folio.	1		1596	A.	L 7
Rarmond (Lord),	Cours Raisonnée de Pratique Civile,	4to.	1	Paris,	1788	A.	L 6
Raymond,	Reports, K. B., C. P., (1694)—6 Geo. 2; (1733)	Folio.	3	London,	1765	A.	O P 6
Raynouard,	Histoire Philosophique et Politique,	8vo.	10	Genève,	1780	B.	T 2
Reeves,	Histoire du Droit Municipal,	8vo.	2 in 1	Paris,	1829	B.	B 2
Remi,	Two Tracts: Americans born before Independence not Aliens,	8vo.	1	London,	1816	E.	B 4
Renouard,	Œuvres complètes de J. Domat; see Donat,						
	Des Droits d'Auteurs,	8vo.	2 in 1	Paris,	1838	B.	D 2
Reusson,	Des Brevets d'Inventions,	8vo.	1	"	1844	B.	D 2
"	Du Douaire et Garde Noble,	4to.	1	"	1724	A.	C 4
"	De la Communauté,	4to.	1	"	1733	A.	C 4
"	De la Subrogation,	4to.	2	"	1743	A.	E 4
Rey,	Institutions Judiciaires de l'Angleterre,	8vo.	1	"	1826	A.	A
Reynaud,	De la Peremption d'Instance,	8vo.	2	"	1837	B.	K 3
Ricard,	Des Douations,	Folio.	2	"	1734	A.	E 7
Richardson,	Attorney's Practice in C. P.,	8vo.	2	Dublin,	1792	A.	L 3
Richer,	De la Mort Civile,	4to.	1	"	1792	L.	L 3
"	Recueil des Arrets de Lamoignon,	4to.	2	Paris,	1755	B.	B 4
Ridgeway,	Reports, Irish Parliament, 1784—1795,	8vo.	3	Dublin,	1783	B.	F 6
Riffé-Caubray et De la Porte,	Pandectes Françaises,	8vo.	15	"	1795—8	A.	P 5
Rics,	Lettres Inédits du Chancelier d'Aguesseau,	4to.	1	"	1806	B.	F 2
Rivière,	De l'Appel,	8vo.	1	"	1823	B.	F 6
Robinson,	On Wills,	8vo.	1	"	1844	B.	C 1
Robinson,	Reports, Supreme Court of Louisiana, 1838—1842,	8vo.	2	Paris, Lyons,	1851	B.	K 4
	Reports, Admiralty, 1841—1843,	8vo.	3	London,	1826	A.	D 4
Robinson, King and Randolph,	Louisiana Annual Reports, 1817—1854,	8vo.	1	New Orleans,	1842—3	A.	N
Rodière,	De la Solidarité,	8vo.	10	London,	1844	A.	R 2
Rodière et Pont,	Du Contrat du Mariage,	8vo.	2	New Orleans,	1847—55	B.	R 4
Rogron,	Code de Procédure Civile Expliqué,	18mo.	1	Paris,	1852	B.	K 3
"	Les Codes Français Expliqué,	4to.	2 in 1	"	1847	B.	C 3
Rogue,	Jurisprudence Consulaire,	18mo.	2	"	1847	B.	K 2
Rolland de Villargues,	Des Substitutions Prohibées par le Code Civil,	8vo.	1	Angers,	1833	A.	G 5
Romlonneau,	Collection Générale des Lois, 1789—1834,	8vo.	70	Paris,	1773	A.	J 3
Roget,	Law of Legacies,	8vo.	1	"	1833—34	A.	D 4
Roquemont,	Manuel Du Droit Ecclésiastique,	8vo.	2	Dublin,	1800	A.	E F G
Roscoe,	On Criminal Evidence,	8vo.	1	London,	1828	A.	D 3
Rose,	Reports, Bankruptcy, 56 Geo. 3, (1816),	12mo.	1	London,	1840	B.	D 4

Roucher,	De la Richesse des Nations; see Smith.						
Rousset,	Memento du Notaire,	18mo.	1	Paris,	1850	B.	K2
Rousilhe,	Les Institutions du Droit de Légitime,	18mo.	2	Avignon,	1778	B.	D3
"	De la Dot,	18mo.	2	Clermont-Ferraud,	1785	B.	C2
"	La Jurisprudence des Donations,	18mo.	3	Avignon,	1785	B.	E4
Routier,	Droit Civil et Coutumier de Normandie,	4to.	1	Rouen,	1742	A.	C6
Rovilliard,	Reliefs Forenses,	4to.	1	Paris,	1610	A.	E6
Russell,	On Crimes,	8vo.	2	London,	1826	A.	M5
"	On Factors and Brokers,	12mo.	1	"	1844	B.	J2
Russell and Ryan,	Crown Cases, 1799—1824,	8vo.	1	"	1825	A.	M4
Ryan and Moody,	Reports at N.P., K.B., C.P., &c., 4 Geo. 4 (1823)—7 Geo. 4 (1826)	8vo.	1	"	1827	A.	P4

Author	Subject	Size	No. of Vols.	Where Published	When	Library	Shelf
Saint Albin,	Logique Judiciaire,	12mo.	1	Paris,	1841	B.	K 3
Saint Elme,	Dictionnaire de la Pénalité,	8vo.	5	"	1824—8	B.	M 2
Saint Joseph,	Concordance entre les Lois Hypothécaires Etrangères,	8vo.	1	"	1847	B.	E 5
	Concordance entre les Codes de Commerce Etrangers, et le Code de Commerce Français,	Folio.	1	Paris,	1851	B.	h 1
Saint Leu,	Coutume de Senlis,	4to.	1	"	1703	A.	D 6
Salkeld,	Reports, K. B., I Wm. and Mary, (1688)—10 Anne, (1712),	Folio.	2	In the Savoy,	1717—24	A.	O 6
Salle,	L'Esprit des Ordonnances de Louis XIV,	4to.	2	Paris,	1758	A.	L 6
"	(Louis XV),	4to.	3	"	1774	B.	E 4
Salligny,	Nouveau Code des Curés,	12mo.	4	"	1790	B.	B 3
Saint,	Coustume de Vitry le Français,	24mo.	1		1651	B.	E 2
Sapey,	Les Etrangers en France,	8vo.	2 in 1	Limoges,	1817	B.	C 3
Saulnier,	Droit de Douane,	8vo.	1	Paris,	1843	B.	B 4
Saunders, Sir E.,	Reports, K. B., Ts (Car. 2 (1667)—24 Car. 2, (1673),	8vo.	1	"	1839	A.	J 2
Savary,	On Pleading and Evidence,	8vo.	2 in 3	London,	1824	B.	O 3
"	Précis sur le Garantie,	8vo.	3	Philadelphia,	1851	A.	L 4
Savary,	D'Economie Politique,	8vo.	1	Niort,	1837	B.	K 4
Scheele,	Cours d'Economie Politique Pratique,	8vo.	1	Paris,	1811	B.	A 3
Scheeks and Lefroy,	Tractatus de Commerciis et Cambio,	Folio.	1		1852	B.	A 3
Scrobell,	Reports, Irish Chancery, 1892—1896,	8vo.	2	Colonie,	1738	B.	J 7
Scott,	Acts of Parliament of General Use, 1649—1656,	Folio.	2	New York,	1808—11	A.	N 2
Sedleu,	New Reports, C. P. and Exc. 5 Wm. 4, (1834)—3 Vic., (1840),	8vo.	8	London,	1658	A.	P 7
Seddons,	Decision of the Sea, or Mare Clausum, (1840)—8 Vic., (1845),	4to.	8	"	1835—11	A.	N 4 5
Serieux,	De Successionibus in Bona Defuncti,	S. 4to.	1		1841—5	A.	N 5
Seyzia,	Les Contrats du Mariage,	18mo.	2	Londini,	1652	A.	A 4
Sergny,	Du Régime Dotal,	8vo.	2	Paris,	1631	A.	U 4
Serrin,	Questions et Traités de Droit Administratif,	8vo.	1	Lyons,	1752	A.	C 2
Sewell,	Œuvres Choisis,	8vo.	3	Paris,	1843	B.	C 4
"	Œuvres Inédits,	8vo.	2	"	1854	B.	A 2
Serrin,	Plaidoyez,	12mo.	4	"	1825	B.	H 3
Shaw,	On Law of Coroner,	8vo.	1	London,	1603—13	B.	H 3
Stratford,	On Bankers' Cheques,	8vo.	1	"	1843	B.	I 1
Shephard,	Law of Railways,	S. 8vo.	1	"	1854	B.	J 4
Shepard,	Law and Practice of Elections,	8vo.	1	"	1853	B.	D 2
Silvela,	Touchstone (of Com. Assurances),	12mo.	1	"	1836	A.	A
Simonnet,	Du Maintien de la Peine de Mort,	8vo.	1	Paris,	1826	A.	D 6
Sirey,	De la Saisine Héréditaire,	8vo.	1	"	1832	B.	M 2
"	Jurisprudence de la Cour le Cassation, 1791—1831,	8vo.	30	"	1852	B.	D 4
"	Table de Recueil des Lois et des Arrets, 1800—1829,	4to.	1	"	1804—31	A.	H & I 4
Sismondi,	Histoire des Français,	8vo.	31	"	1821—44	B.	D 1

Author	Title	Vols.	Size	Place	Date	Shelf
Sismondi,	Études sur les Constitutions des Peuples Libres,	3	8vo.	Paris,	1836—8	B. A 3
Smith,	De la Richesse des Nations,	5	8vo.	"	1795	B. A 2
	On Government Commissions,	1	8vo.	London,	1849	A. A 4
Société de Jurisconsultes,	Annales du Barreau Français, (ancien)	7	8vo.	Paris,	1829—35	A. H 1
"	" (moderne)	13	Folio.	"	1835—47	A. H 1
Sofio,	Nouveau Recueil des Arrêts du Parlement de Paris, 1640—1682,	1	8vo.	"	1682	B. I 7
Solon,	Des Hypothèques,	2 in 1	18mo.	Toulouse,	1835	B. K 3
Sombatges,	Théorie sur la Nullité,	1	Folio.	Paris,	1761	B. h 1
Sorquet,	Vie Foraine des Temps Legaux, de Droit, et de Procédure,	2	8vo.	"	1844	B. D 3
Sourdat,	De la Responsabilité,	2	8vo.	"	1852	A. D 2
Sheetz,	On Specification,	1	8vo.	London,	1847	B. P 4
Starkie,	Reports at N. P., K. B. & C. P., 55 Geo. 3 (1814)—59 Geo. 3 (1819)	1	8vo.	"	1817—20	A. L 5
Stephen,	On Law of Evidence,	4	8vo.	"	1833	B. a 1
"	Commentaries on Laws of England,	1	8vo.	"	1853	A. b 1
Stephens and Norton,	Modern Law Catalogue,	1	12mo.	"	1853	A. J 2
Story,	On Bailments,	1	8vo.	Cambridge,	1832	B. A 4
"	On Constitution of United States,	3	8vo.	Boston, Cambridge,	1833	A. A 4
"	On Conflict of Laws,	2 in 1	8vo.	Boston,	1834	B. A 5
"	Constitution Fédérale des États-Unis,	1	8vo.	Paris,	1843	B. J 5
"	On Contracts,	1	8vo.	Boston,	1847	B. J 3
"	On Partnership,	1	8vo.	"	1850	B. J 3
"	On Agency,	1	8vo.	"	1851	B. J 4
"	On Promissory Notes,	1	8vo.	"	1851	B. A 4
"	On Conflict of Laws,	1	8vo.	"	1852	B. J 4
"	On Bills of Exchange,	1	8vo.	"	1853	A. N 6
Strange, Sir J.,	Reports, Chancery, K. B., C. P. and Exc., 2 Geo. 1, (1716)—21 Geo. 2, (1749)	2	Folio.	Dublin,	1756	A. U 5
Sam.,	Historia Juris,	1	4to.	Jena,	1718	A. c 4
Stuart,	Reports, Lower Canada,	1	8vo.	Quebec,	1834	A. M 4
Sugden and Talmash,	Crown Companion,	1	8vo.	London,	1790	A. E 6
Sugden,	Law of Vendors and Purchasers,	2	8vo.	"	1808	A. E 6
"	On Powers,	1	8vo.	"	1836	B. D 3
"	On the New Statutes,	1	8vo.	"	1852	B. D 4
Swinburne,	On Wills,	1	8vo.	Dublin,	1793	B.

Author.	Subject.	Size.	No. of Vols.	Where Published.	When.	Library.	Shelf.
Talandier,	Des Abseus,	8vo.	1	Paris,	1831	B.	B 4
"	De l'Appel,	8vo.	1	"	1839	B.	K 4
Talbot, Lord Ch.,	Cases in Equity, 7 Geo. 2, 1734.	Folio.	1	In the Savoy,	1753	A.	N 6
Tapping,	On Mandamus,	8vo.	1	London,	1848	B.	L 3
Tarbe,	Des Poids et Mesures,	18mo.	1	Paris,	1845	B.	D 2
Taunton,	Reports, C. P., 48 Geo. 3 (1808)—59 Geo. 3 (1819)	8vo.	8	London,	1814—23	A.	N 3
Taylor,	On the Civil Law,	4to.	1	"	1755	A.	U 6
"	Reports, Ny., Can., K. B., 4 Geo. 4 (1824)—8 Geo. 4 (1828)	8vo.	1	York, U. C.,	1828	A.	c
"	Book of Rights,	12mo.	1	London,	1833	B.	
"	On Difference between Law of England and Scotland relating to Contracts,						
Terrasson,	Œuvres,	8vo.	1	London,	1849	B.	J 5
Teulet,	Recueil des Constitutions Françaises, 1791—1851,	4to.	1	Paris,	1737	B.	G 6
Teulet, D'Auvilliers et Sulpicy,	Les Codes Français,	12mo.	2	"	1851	B.	A 2
Thibault,	Des Crices,	4to.	2 in 1	"	1850	B.	G 5
Thaumassière,	Nouveau Commentaires sur les Coutumes; see De la Thaumassière.	4to.		"	1760	B.	K 6
Tidd.	Practice of Courts of K. B. and C. P.,	8vo.	2	London,	1828	A.	L 4
Tillard,	Forms of Proceedings in K. B., C. P., and Exc.,	8vo.	1	"	1828	A.	L 5
Tisso?,	Des Actes Dissolutifs de Communauté,	8vo.	1	Paris,	1831	B.	C 1
	Les Douze Livres du Code de Justinien,	4to.	4	Metz,	1807—10	A.	U 6
	Principes Métaphysiques du Droit; see Kant.						
Tolliure et Boilet,	Ferrière Moderne.	8vo.	2 in 1	Paris,	1841	B.	K 4
Toubeau,	Institutes du Droit Consulaire,	4to.	1	"	1700	B.	J 6
Toullier,	Droit Civil Français,	8vo.	15	"	1830—4	A.	F 3
Tournel,	Arrêts Notables.	Folio.	2	"	1631	A.	J 7
Tourneux et Angers,	Revue de Législation en Bas Canada; see LeTourneux.						
Troncon,	Droit Français et Coutume de Paris,	Folio.	1	Paris,	1643	A.	D 7
	Commentaire sur la Coutume de Paris,	Folio.	1	"	1652	A.	C 7
	Droit Français et Coutume de Paris,	8vo.	5	"	1664	A.	D 7
Troplong,	Droit Civil Français,	8vo.	2	Paris,	1833—4	A.	F 4
"	Droit Civil—Prescription,	8vo.	2	"	1838	A.	F 4
"	" —Exchange and Lonage,	8vo.	2	"	1840—4	A.	F 4
"	" De Société,	8vo.	2	"	1843	A.	F 4
"	" Du Prêt,	8vo.	4	"	1845	A.	F 4
"	" Des Privilèges et Hypothèques,	8vo.	2	"	1845	A.	F 4
"	" De la Vente,	8vo.	1	"	1845	A.	F 4
"	" Du Cautionnement,	8vo.	1	"	1846	A.	F 4
"	" Du Mandat,	8vo.	1	"	1846	A.	F 4
"	" Du Nantissement,	8vo.	1	"	1857	A.	F 4
"	" De la Contrainte par Corps,	8vo.	1	"	1847	A.	F 4
"	" Du Contrat de Mariage,	8vo.	4	"	1850	A.	F 4

						B.	F 4
Troplong, ...	De l'Influence du Christianisme sur le Droit Civil des Romains,..	8vo.	1	Paris, ...	1843		
Trower, ...	On Fusion of Law and Equity,...............	8vo.	1	London, ...	1851		
Tudertinus, ...	Tractatus de Juramento Litis, &c.; see Carroceius.						

Author.	Subject.	Size.	No. of Vols.	Where Published.	When.	Library.	Shelf.
United Kingdom,	British Acts, 6 Anne (1708)—32 Geo. 2 (1759)	18mo.	21	Edinburgh,	1718	A.	T 1
"	Commons Journals, 1 Ed. 6 (1547)—54 Geo. 3 (1813)	Folio.	68			A.	l m n o p q
"	General Index to ditto, 1800,	Folio.	6			A.	r
"	Statutes at Large—Magna Charta—41 Geo. 3 (1801)	4to.	18	London,	1763	A.	l m
"	Index to ditto, " 49 Geo. 3 ( )	4to.	1	"		A.	r
"	Statutes at Large, 41 Geo. 3 (1801)—13 Vic. (1849)	4to.	19	"	1814	A.	m
"	" 13 Vic. (1850)—17 Vic. (1853)	4to.	2 in 4	"	1830—3	A.	m n
"	" 7 and 8 Vic., and 8 and 9 Vic.,	4to.	1	"	1845	A.	o n
United States,	Reports from Committees of House of Commons, 1572—1715,	Folio.	4			A.	r
Upper Canada,	Rotuli Parliamentorum, Ed. 1 ( )—Ed. 6 ( )	Folio.	6			A.	l
	Acts of 3rd Congress,	8vo.	1	Philadelphia,	1795	A.	R 6
	Revised Statutes ; see Canada,						
Urwin,	Observations sur le Code Henry,	12mo.	1	Paris,	1617	B.	E 2

Author.	Subject.	Size.	No. of Vols.	Where Published.	When.	Library.	Shelf.
Valette,	De l'Inscription en Matière de Privilèges,	8vo.	1	Paris,	1843	B.	E 5
Valin,	Nouveau Commentaire sur Ordonnance de la Marine,	4to.	2	Rochelle,	1766	A.	J 6
"	Commentaire sur l'Ordonnance de la Marine,	4to.	1	Paris et Poitiers,	1829	B.	J 6
Vanhuffel,	Contrat de Louage et de Dépôt, appliqué aux Voituriers, &c.,	8vo.	1	Paris,	1841	B.	C 1
Van Leeuwen,	Corpus Juris Civilis,	Folio.	1	Amstelodami,	1663	A.	R 7
Vasserot,	Nouveau Manuel des Experts,	8vo.	1	Paris,	1845	B.	K 3
Vattel,	Droit des Gens,	8vo.	2	Paris,	1839	A.	A 5
Vazeille,	Du Mariage et Puissance Maritale,	8vo.	2	"	1825	B.	C 3
"	Des Prescriptions,	8vo.	2	"	1832	B.	C 4
"	Conférence des Commentaires du Code Civil sur les Successions, &c	8vo.	3	Clermont-Ferrand,	1837	B.	D 4
Vauzelles,	Bacon, Justice Universelle; see Bacon.						
Vernon,	Revised Statutes,	8vo.	1	Burlington,	1840	A.	R 6
Vernon,	Cases in Chancery, 1680—1718,	Folio.	2	In the Savoy,	1726	A.	N 6
Vesey,	Reports, Chancery, 1746—1755, &c	8vo.	in 3	London,	1788	A.	N 1
Vesey, Jr.,	29 Geo. 3 (1789)—58 Geo. 3 (1817),	8vo.	20	"	1801—22	A.	N 1 & 2
Vesey and Beames,	53 Geo. 3 (1812)—54 Geo. 3 (1814),	8vo.	2	"	1818	A.	N 2
Vincens,	De la Législation Commerciale,	8vo.	2	Paris,	1821	A.	J 4
Vincent,	Voyage de Néarque,	4to.	1	"	1800	A.	g
"	Sur la Loi Musulmane,	Folio.	1	"	1842	B.	M 2
Viner,	Abridgment of Law and Equity,	Folio.	21	Aldershot,	1746—5	A.	N O 7
Vinnius,	Commentarius,	4to.	1	Lugduni Batavorum,	1726	A.	U 5
Virgilius,	Opera,	8vo.	1	Edinburgh,	1820	A.	U 1
Voetius,	Commentarius ad Pandectas,	8vo.	1—7	Halæ,	1776—80	A.	U 2

Author.	Subject.	Size.	No. of Vols.	Where Published.	When.	Library.	Shelf.
Walker,	Collection des Lois, &c., antérieures à 1789,	8vo.	5	Paris,	1835—7	B.	D
Warnkœnig,	Corpus Juris Romani,	8vo.	3	Leodii,	1825—9	A.	U 3
Watkins,	On Conveyancing,	8vo.	1	London,	1833	A.	D 6
Waterman,	On New Trials,	8vo.	3	New York,	1855	A.	L 4
Webster,	Works,	8vo.	6	Boston,	1833	A.	H 2
"	On the New Patent Law,	12mo.	1	London,	1844	A.	D 2
Wendell,	Reports, Supreme Court of New York, 1828—1841,	8vo.	in 26	Albany,	1829—42	A.	Q 34
Wentworth,	On Pleading,	8vo.	10	Dublin,	1799	A.	L 4
Weskett,	On Insurance,	8vo.	1	London,	1781	A.	J 7
West,	Precedents, or Symboleography,	Folio.	1	London,	1632	A.	L 3
Weston,	Reports, Supreme Court of Vermont, 1839 and 1840,	S. 4to.	1	Burlington,	1841	A.	R 1
Wheaton,	Reports, Supreme Court of United States, 1816—1827,	8vo.	12	Philadelphia & N. York,	1816—27	A.	Q
"	On International Law,	8vo.	2	London,	1836	B.	A 4
"	Elements du Droit International,	8vo.	2 in 1	Leipzig,	1852	B.	A 4
Wharton,	Histoire des Progrès du Droit des Gens,	8vo.	2 in 1	"	1853	B.	A 5
Wicksteed,	Roman Catholic Statute Law,	8vo.	1	London,	1848	B.	g
"	Index to Statutes of Lower Canada,	8vo.	1	Toronto,	1851	B.	B 3
Williams,	Reports, Chancery, 1695—1121,	8vo.	1	Upper Canada,	1857	A.	c 1
"	Justice of the Peace,	Folio.	in 2		1856	A.	c 1
"	Digest of Statute Law—Magna Charta—18 Geo. 3,	8vo.	5	In the Savoy,	1746	A.	N 6
Wilson,	On Executors,	8vo.	2	London,	1793	A.	M 1
Wise,	Reports, K. B. and C. P., 16 Geo. 3 (1742)—14 Geo. 3 (1774)	8vo.	2		1899	A.	b 1
Wilmot,	On Riots,	Folio.	2		1832	A.	D 4
Wolowski et al.,	On Burglary,	12mo.	1		1779	A.	P 6
"	Revue de Législation et de Jurisprudence, 1834—1832,	8vo.	1		1848	B.	M 2
Wood,	Revue Critique " 1853—1856,	8vo.	47 in 20	Paris,	1851	B.	M 2
Woodfall,	(Institute of the) Laws of England,	8vo.	7	"	1835—33	B.	S 4
Woolrych,	On Landlord and Tenant,	Folio.	1	In the Savoy,	1853—56	B.	T 4
"	On Mischenacanours,	8vo.	1	London,	1724	A.	Q 7
"	On Waters,	12mo.	1	"	1819	A.	C 1
		8vo.	1	"	1842	B.	M 2
					1851	B.	

Author.	Subject.	Size.	No. of Vols.	Where Published.	When.	Library.	Shelf.
Yelverton, Sir H.,	Reports, K. B., 4 Eliz., (1601)—10 Jas., (1612)	8vo.	1	Dublin,	1792	A.	O 3

Author.	Subject.	Size.	No. of Vols.	Where Published.	When.	Library.	Shelf.
Zachariæ,	Cours de Droit Civil Français,	8vo.	5	Strasbourg,	1839—46	B.	F 5